VENUS & AD

She's love, she loves, and yet she is not lov'd.
Narrator, line 610

Shakespearean
AUTHORSHIP TRUST

This edition sponsored by the Shakespearean Authorship Trust.
www.ShakespeareanAuthorshipTrust.com
WhoWroteShakespeare.substack.com

Performed at the Marylebone Theatre, London,
with Mark Rylance as Narrator, Kristin Scott Thomas as Venus,
and Johnny Flynn as Adonis, with Ian Rickson directing.

November 17, 2024

VENUS & ADONIS

SHAKESPEARE

edited, designed, and produced by

Robin Williams

....

iREAD
SHAKESPEARE
READERS' EDITIONS

Venus and Adonis, **by Shakespeare**
Edited, designed, and produced by Robin Williams, Ph.D.
iReadShakespeare *Readers' Edition*
©2024 Robin Williams and iReadShakespeare

Published by iReadShakespeare
www.iReadShakespeare.org

The text in this book is from the 1593 quarto (small
paperback edition). With some exceptions, this book
uses the punctuation found in the 1593 quarto; it also
maintains the original spellings of words such as
my self and *to-day*. Explanations of words reflect the
meanings they had at the time they were written, using
the Oxford English Dictionary (OED).

The cover illustration is painted by Titian (c. 1488–1576, lived
to 88 years old) of the Venetian school of art. There are various
versions of this painting, most of them with Adonis bare-headed.
This particular version of Adonis wearing a hat, or bonnet,
is not known to have been in England so it is a puzzlement if
William Shaksper of Stratford-upon-Avon could have seen it.
It is believed that several copies of Adonis in the bonnet were
in Titian's studio in Venice, with originals perhaps in Spain,
Russia, or Sweden.

The digital image used on the cover is in the public domain.

This book has been tested, with grateful appreciation, .
by the iReadShakespeare online group. And a special
thank-you to Jay Ann Martin.

Printed and bound in the United States.

*Shakespeare has created a powerful poetic
variation on an ancient myth that is
at the same time a rhetorical tour de force.*
David Bevington

Contents

Plays have a double life:
in the mind as read,
and on the stage as acted.

Reading a play and seeing it acted
are two different but equally valid
and valuable experiences.

R. A. Foakes (1923–2013)

Welcome to the Readers' Edition

The first printed edition of the collected works of Shakespeare is called the First Folio, published in 1623. The first three words in the edition are "To the **Reader,**" and the dedication is "To the Great Variety of **Readers.**" It is not dedicated to actors.

The United States of America has a long history of Shakespeare reading groups, from private family readings in parlors and log cabins to the astounding Woman's Club movement that began in the mid-nineteenth century and spread Shakespeare across the country.

> The study [of Shakespeare] is rarely given up, and new clubs are constantly formed to undertake it. Shakespeare Clubs all devote some time to book reviews, current events, and some new voice of to-day, for the study of Shakespeare stimulates the mind, broadens and uplifts it, and gives an interest in all vital questions, but to the greatest study of all, all return with renewed zeal.
>
> Jennie June Cunningham Croly
> *History of the Woman's Club Movement in America,* 1898

The millions of early readers had no credentialed scholar to guide them nor actor to interpret the text for them—they jumped in and read aloud and discussed and argued and pondered and reread. We are finally seeing a robust return to this time-honored tradition, and this Readers' Edition is in full support. With just enough explanations of words and a few call-outs to lines of text that warrant special attention, it encourages *readers* to spend time with this remarkable poetic drama and discover its gems for *yourselves*.

Whether your group has been around for a century or is brand new, kudos to you for building a community of Shakespeare readers—out loud and in community!

Robin Williams

If you're new to *reading* Shakespeare

Here are a few tips on **reading** Shakespeare **aloud,** in case you are unfamiliar with the process. If you take a few minutes to understand these issues, I guarantee it will help immensely.

Thee or You?

The use of *thee* and *thou* and phrases such as *thou dost* can be confusing when reading Shakespeare.

YOU and YOUR *vs.* THEE and THOU

Most languages have different forms of "you"—a familiar and a formal form. In Shakespeare's time, this difference in English was still in use.

You is formal and respectful; it is used when speaking to someone older or higher in rank. It is occasionally used with a kind of passive-aggressive pseudo-respect attitude.

You is also *thou* in plural, as when a nobleman addresses a crowd of peasants.

Thou and **thee** is informal or derogatory. It is used when speaking to people with whom you are intimate, such as your husband when you are in private, or to God. **Thou** is more often used to speak to people beneath your rank— children, servants, rogues. **Thou** can be used to put someone in their place or denigrate someone to whom you *should* be using **you.**

Verbs attached to **thou** change a little—they have the letters *t, st,* or *est* added at the end. Below is an easy chart. Simply change *thou* to *you* and remove the *t, st,* or *est* from the verb (and *hast = have*).

thou art	*thou dost*	*thou canst*	*thou sayest*	*thou hast*
↓	↓	↓	↓	↓
you are	*you do*	*you can*	*you say*	*you have*

You will also see **hath** and **doth** (**doth** has the same **o** sound as is *does;* it is not an *ah* sound). **Hath** and **doth** simply mean **has** and **does** (3rd person).

His eye so full hath fed	*Now doth she stroke his cheek*
Quick desire hath caught him	*Swelling passion doth prevent a pause*
When he hath ceased his noise	*Her blood doth boil*

Thee is a singular object, so whenever you see **thee,** substitute **you** in your mind.
   *Hope makes **thee** ridiculous.*

Thy and **thine** mean **your** (use *thine* if the following word starts with a vowel).
   thy heart   thine own heart

So whenever you see *thee, thy, thine, thou,* etc., just think *you* or *your.*

To native English speakers who have no experience with other languages, the use of *thee* or *you* can seem arbitrary. But to Shakespeare's audience (as it is in most languages still today), the difference was enormous. Eventually you will start noticing which form of address characters use; think about what Shakespeare is trying to tell you with that information.

The purpose: *In general,* when a character uses *thee* or *thou,* they are either being intimate or disrespectful; when using *you* and *your,* they are being formal or respectful (or sometimes passive-aggressively formal). The distinction tells us so much about the attitude of the characters and their relationships.

Verse, blank verse, rhymed verse

You can completely skip this information if you like! But if you have an interest in knowing the basics of iambic pentameter, then here is a *very* basic primer.

VERSE

Most lines of any Shakespeare play have ten (sometimes eleven) syllables; these lines are called **verse.** You can tell when the lines are in verse because every line starts with a capital letter (and has ten syllables). Each line also has a definite pattern of sound, like a heartbeat, with an emphasis on the *bum:*

> ba **BUM** · ba **BUM** · ba **BUM** · ba **BUM** · ba **BUM**

Technically, each **ba BUM** is called an *iamb,* which is one *foot* in a line of poetry. Because there are five (*pénte* in Greek) iambs in each line, Shakespeare's verse is called *iambic pentameter.*

> If **love** have **lent** you **twen**ty t**hou**sand **tongues,**
> And **ev**ery **tongue** more **mo**ving **than** your **own**

This is what forces Shakespeare to sometimes put words in an odd order, and also to add or delete syllables by using accent marks and apostrophes (see pages 10–11)—so the words will fit into the rhythm of the line. There are often intentional disruptions in an iambic pentameter line (including an eleventh syllable or disrupted meter), but that's another fascinating discussion.

BLANK VERSE AND PROSE

Blank verse is simply lines of verse that don't rhyme. Most of the text in all the plays is in blank verse. There is, of course, plenty of **prose,** which is plain old speaking in regular lines; the first letters of each line are not capitalized, and the lines are not limited to ten syllables.

RHYMED VERSE

It is **verse** that **rhymes,** of course. *Venus and Adonis* is in **rhymed verse.** In a Shakespearean play, which is mostly blank verse, Shakespeare uses rhyme very specifically, which is another fascinating discussion.

Apostrophes

If you are new to reading Shakespeare aloud, do *not* worry about pronouncing words specifically. The apostrophes are explained here merely so they don't confuse you. You'll find, as you read more and more Shakespearean works, that you will naturally start pronouncing odd words more confidently.

When you see an **apostrophe,** it indicates that **a letter or two** (a syllable, actually) has been **left out.** This is not unusual in English: we write *can't* instead of *cannot;* the apostrophe in *can't* indicates that we are leaving out the letters *no*. The apostrophe in *isn't* indicates the o is missing.

Take a sentence such as: *With her I lived in joy*. I have heard many Readers pronounce this as: *With her I liv-ed in joy,* mistakenly believing they are supposed to do a "Shakespearean" thing and pronounce *lived* as *liv-ed*. This is perfectly okay, but the Reader feels insecure not knowing what is actually correct. To prevent this insecure feeling, I have left the text the way it was set in the first printed version of this poem, including the apostrophes, so you can see what Shakespeare intended and not get confused.

Shakespeare's purpose with the apostrophes is to make sure a line has the correct number of syllables for the meter (as briefly introduced on page 9).

In the poem, you will find words like this:

> *'tis* = it is. The letter *i* is missing and the two words are smushed together, just like *does not* into *doesn't*.

> *dispos'd* = disposed. The apostrophe is Shakespeare's way of reminding you **not** to add the *ed* as a syllable. You wouldn't automatically add the *ed* sound in English today anyway, but with the apostrophe, you won't have to wonder how to pronounce it.

> *threat'ning* = threat**e**ning, spoken in two syllables instead of three.

> *ta'en* = ta**k**en; the *k* is missing so it is one syllable. Feel free to pronounce it as *taken*.

> *th' extremity* = the apostrophe deletes the **e**; *th'* rolls onto the *e* in *extremity*. Thus the phrase is four syllables instead of five.

> *wild wat'ry seas* = wild wat**e**ry seas, but *wat'ry* has two syllables, not three.

Of course, you will also find apostrophes in possessive words, as usual:

> *I am a woman's man.*

🍁 **To summarize:** When you see an **apostrophe** where a letter is missing, it means you ***do not*** pronounce the missing letter. (But if you're uncomfortable doing that, feel free to actually pronounce it however you like, until you become accustomed to speaking Shakespearean language. It'll grow on you.)

Accent marks

Apostrophes are used to *delete* syllables, or at least make sure we don't pronounce them, whereas **accent marks** are used to create **extra** syllables.

An **accent mark** over a vowel, as in *disturbèd,* indicates that you **do** pronounce that syllable where you otherwise might not; *disturbèd* is three syllables instead of two: *dis turb ed.*

Most lines in any Shakespeare play are ten syllables long (see page 9). Sometimes an extra syllable has to be forced into the line, as in this one:

> *The steed is stallèd up, and even now*

Without the accent mark, we would naturally pronounce *stalled* as *stall'd,* with one syllable. The accent mark tells us Shakespeare wants an extra syllable in that position: *stall-ed.* This is another example:

> *Controlling what he was controllèd with*

In this book when you see an accent mark, you can pronounce that syllable.

Occasionally the accent mark tells you to put the emphasis on a syllable other than the one you are accustomed to:

> *This ill presàge advisedly she marks*

But don't worry about it!

Do *not* worry about pronouncing the accented syllables or deleting the syllables where there is an apostrophe until you feel comfortable! The purpose of these explanations is simply so you will know what's going on with the markings.

When you get to a point where you are fascinated with how Shakespeare's meter works and what it tells you, then you can worry about it.

No. of lines	Characters
495	**Venus,** the Goddess of Love
88	**Adonis,** a young mortal, male
611	**Narrator**

Who are Venus and Adonis?

Venus, also known by her Greek name, Aphrodite, is the ancient Goddess of love, lust, sex, fertility, beauty. Her symbols are also lusty: sparrows, dolphins, swans, bees, rabbits.

Venus was married to Vulcan/Hephaestus but had an affair with **Mars**/Ares, as she tells us in lines 97–112 (she also had numerous other lovers). Venus and Mars had a child, **Cupid,** also called Love, who is frequently mentioned (with a capital L) in this poem.

Adonis, as Pseudo-Apollodorus tells us in *Bibliotheca* (first century CE) is the child of **Myrrha** (Smyrna in Greek) and her father. Venus/Aphrodite was wrathful because Myrrha did not worship the Goddess appropriately, so Venus cursed Myrrha to desperately lust for her own father; she slept with him for twelve nights. When her father discovered with whom he was sleeping, he chased Myrrha with his sword—but the Gods took pity and turned her into a myrrh tree before he could kill her. Myrrha was pregnant with her father's child when she transformed into the tree, and nine months later the tree gave birth— to **Adonis.** The resin secreted from a myrrh tree are the tears she still weeps.

In the classical age of Europe, **Adonis** is considered the ideal of manly beauty, and **Venus** as female beauty.

Motifs and themes to watch for

Shakespeare always uses motifs (repetitive patterns) or themes (universal ideas) to weave a play or long poem together. Ask each other, "why?"

Red vs. white: The contrast or connection between these two colors appear in myriad situations. Every time you notice it, think about what the author is comparing or contrasting.

Love vs. lust The poem repeatedly contrasts Love as gentle, comforting, and peaceful, while Lust is violent, boisterous, and selfish.

Hunter vs. prey Who is the hunter? Who is the prey? Note the vicious imagery of both lust and hunting.

About this poem

When *Venus and Adonis* appeared in the bookstalls of St. Paul's in the spring of 1593, it caused an immediate sensation. No one had ever written a character quite like the fleshy, frustrated Goddess who flung herself at the reticent Adonis. While the story was familiar from Ovid's *Metamorphoses,* this version incorporated elements of the poet's *Amores* and *Art of Love (Ars Amatoria,* a manual for seduction), considered too scandalous for schoolboys.

It was convention in Elizabethan poetry that classical Goddesses represented Queen Elizabeth. Period readers identified the fallen Adonis with Sir Philip Sidney, the brilliant courtier and writer who died in 1586 fighting the Spanish. The nature of his fatal wound and Sidney's well-known quarrel with Edward de Vere, 17th Earl of Oxford, whose heraldic symbol was a blue boar, made the match. Sidney's refusal to court the Queen as she wished made the identification of Venus with Elizabeth both unthinkable and unavoidable. And her new infatuation with Robert Devereux, the dashing young Earl of Essex who inherited Sidney's sword and married his widow, was already replaying the tragic story. And yet, for all the titillating sexual content and the political topicality, the poem was also a sophisticated entry into the literary debate over the role of literature inspired by Sidney's essay, "The Defense of Poesy."

Sidney defended writers and dramatists from Puritan critics who accused them of corrupting audiences by celebrating the "strumpet Venus." *Venus and Adonis* fulfilled Sidney's vision of an English vernacular literature that would "delight and inspire," defying the Puritan impulse to ban poetry and theater.

The author was not identified on the title page, but the dedication to Henry Wriothesley, Earl of Southampton, bore a name familiar to us but new to Elizabethan audiences: "William Shakespeare."

With this "first heir of my invention," Shakespeare claims the mantles of both Ovid and Sidney and grimly anticipated the political and cultural battle between Essex and Cecil that defined the last years of Elizabeth's reign. It was the best-selling work of the age.

David W. Richardson, Ph.D.
DavidWRichardson.substack.com

Southampton as "patron"

Although the patronage of Southampton is part of the mythical legend surrounding the man named William Shakespeare, there is actually not a single, slight piece of documented evidence that Henry Wriothesley, the Earl of Southampton, patronized Shakespeare in any way. It is well-documented that authors dedicated works to noblemen hoping (fishing) for some sort of acknowledgment or monetary recognition. There are records of authors receiving £5 or sometimes £10, but no records that Shakespeare received anything from Southampton, nor that he even acknowledged Shakespeare's existence.

VENVS AND ADONIS

*Vilia miretur vulgus: mihi flauus Apollo
Pocula Castalia plena ministret aqua.*

LONDON

Imprinted by Richard Field, and are to be sold at
the signe of the white Greyhound in
Paules Church-yard.
1593.

The Latin states: *The common people are surprised: Apollo is fair to me
Castalia pours a cup full of water.*

It is anciently written that the nymph Castalia threw herself
into a spring near the oracle of Delphi to escape being raped
by Apollo, the god of oracles, music, art, and knowledge. Thus
the water inspires the wisdom of poetry to those who drink it.

TO THE RIGHT HONORABLE
Henrie VVriothesley, Earle of Southampton,
and Baron of Titchfield.

Right Honourable, I know not how I shall offend in
dedicating my unpolisht lines to your Lordship, nor
how the worlde vvill censure mee for choosing so
strong a proppe to support so vveake a burthen,
onelye if your Honour seeme but pleased, I ac-
count my selfe highly praised, and vowe to take aduantage of all
idle houres, till I haue honoured you vvith some grauer labour. But
if the first heire of my inuention proue deformed, I shall be sorie it
had so noble a god-father : and neuer after eare so barren a land,
for feare it yeeld me still so bad a haruest, I leaue it to your Honourable suruey, and your Honor to your hearts content, vvhich I vvish
may alvvaies ansuvere your ovvne vvish, and the vvorlds hope-
full expectation.

Your Honors in all dutie,

William Shakespeare.

The dedication reads: TO THE RIGHT HONORABLE Henry Wriothesley, Earl of Southampton, and Baron of Titchfield.

Right Honourable,

I know not how I shall offend in dedicating my unpolish'd lines to Your Lordship, nor how the world will censure me for choosing so strong a prop to support so weak a burden, only if your Honour seem but pleased, I account my self highly praised, and vow to take advantage of all idle hours, till I have honoured you with some graver labour. But if **the first heir of my invention** prove deformed, I shall be sorry it had so noble a god-father: and never after ear so barren a land, for fear it yield me still so bad a harvest. I leave it to your honourable survey, and Your Honour to your heart's content, which I wish may always answer your own wish, and the world's hopeful expectation.

Your Honor's in all duty,
William Shakespeare.

Guide to details of the page

Venus and Adonis • LINES 355–390

Gloss dot *indicates this word is glossed.*

355	O what a war of looks was then between them:	
356	Her eyes, petitioners˙ to his eyes suing,	*beggars; begging*
357	His eyes saw her eyes, as˙ they had not seen them;	*as if*
358	Her eyes woo'd still, his eyes disdain'd the wooing:	
359	And all this dumb˙ play had his acts made plain	*silent*
360	With tears which, chorus-like, her eyes did rain.	

Explanatory notes. *Sometimes these are questions for your reading group.*

*A dumb play, or dumb show (as in Hamlet), is a performance without words. Venus's **tears** act as a **chorus** to interpret the action.*

Gloss *(definition): You can **substitute** the gloss for the word with the **gloss dot**.*

361	Full gently now she takes him by the hand,	
362	A lily prison'd in a jail of snow,	
363	Or ivory in an alabaster band˙;	*bond*
364	So white a friend engirts˙ so white a foe.	*surrounds*
365	This beauteous combat, willful and unwilling,	
366	Show'd like two silver doves that sit a-billing.	

*Here **the engine** is her tongue.*

Multiple glosses *in one line are separated by **semicolons**.*

*Phrases in **parentheses** are explanations rather than definitions.*

367	Once more the engine of her thoughts began:	
368	"O fairest mover on this mortal round,˙	*Earth*
369	Would˙ thou wert as I am, and I a man,	*I wish*
370	My heart all whole as thine, thy heart my˙ wound.	*feeling my*
371	For one sweet look, thy help I would assure thee,	
372	Though nothing but my body's bane˙ would cure thee."	*ruin*

Room to write *your own **notes**.*

373	"Give me my hand," saith he, "why dost thou feel˙ it?"	*hang on to*
374	"Give me my heart," saith she, "and thou shalt have it.˙	*your hand*
375	O give it me, lest thy hard heart do steel˙ it,	*harden*
376	And being steel'd, soft sighs can never grave˙ it.	*engrave on*
377	Then love's deep groans I never shall regard,	
378	Because Adonis' heart hath made mine hard."	

Red *line numbers indicate **Venus** is speaking.* **Blue** *numbers are **Adonis**.* **Black** *are the **Narrator**.*

379	"For shame," he cries, "let go, and let me go;	
380	My day's delight is past, my horse is gone,	
381	And 'tis your fault I am bereft˙ him so.	*deprived of*
382	I pray you, hence,˙ and leave me here alone,	*go away*
383	For all my mind, my thought, my busy care,	
384	Is how to get my palfrey˙ from the mare."	*saddle horse*

*Every line is **numbered** so those reading the same book can refer quickly and easily to specific lines.*

385	Thus she replies, "Thy palfrey, as he should,	
386	Welcomes the warm approach of sweet desire;	
387	Affection˙ is a coal that must be cool'd,	*passion*
388	Else suffer'd,˙ it will set the heart on fire.	*allowed to burn*
389	The sea hath bounds, but deep desire hath none;	
390	Therefore no marvel though thy horse be gone.	

*There is **a lot of the poem text** on the double-page spread so you can see a good deal of the progress at one time.*

VENUS & ADONIS

*Phoebus is the **Sun** God who takes leave of the Goddess of the **Morn**, Aurora, to travel across the sky. This first stanza sums up the poem.*

1 Even as the Sun with purple-color'd˙ face   *blushing*
2 Had ta'en his last leave of the weeping˙ Morn,   *dewy*
3 Rose-cheek'd Adonis hied˙ him to the chase.   *hurried*
4 Hunting he lov'd, but love he laugh'd to scorn.
5   Sick-thoughted˙ Venus makes amain˙ unto him,   *lovesick; quickly*
6   And like a bold-fac'd suitor, 'gins to woo him.

7 "Thrice fairer than my self," thus she began,
8 "The field's chief flower, sweet above compare,

*Adonis is a **stain** in that his own beauty makes **all nymphs** look inferior.*

9 Stain to all nymphs, more lovely than a man,
10 More white and red than doves or roses are:
11   Nature,˙ that made thee, with her self at strife,   *Mother Nature*
12   Saith that the *world* hath ending with thy life.˙   *life's end*

13 "Vouchsafe,˙ thou wonder, to alight thy steed,   *grant me*
14 And rein his proud head to the saddle-bow;
15 If thou wilt deign this favor, for thy meed˙   *reward*
16 A thousand honey secrets shalt thou know.
17   Here, come and sit, where never serpent hisses,
18   And being set, I'll smother thee with kisses.

19 "And yet not cloy thy lips with loath'd satiety,˙   *over-indulgence*
20 But rather famish them amid their plenty,
21 Making them red and pale, with fresh variety—
22 Ten kisses short as one, one long as twenty:
23   A summer's day will seem an hour but short,
24   Being wasted in such time-beguiling sport."

25 With this she seizeth on his sweating palm,
26 The precedent˙ of pith˙ and livelihood,   *sign; vigor*
27 And trembling in her passion, calls it balm,
28 Earth's sovereign salve, to do a Goddess good.
29   Being so enrag'd,˙ desire doth lend her force,   *passionate*
30   Courageously˙ to pluck him from his horse.   *lustfully*

31	Over one arm the lusty courser's˙ rein,	*stallion's*
32	Under her other was the tender boy,	
33	Who blush'd and pouted in a dull disdain,	
34	With leaden appetite, unapt˙ to toy˙—	*unsuited; flirt*
35	She, red and hot as coals of glowing fire;	
36	He, red for shame, but frosty in desire.	
37	The studded bridle on a ragged bough	
38	Nimbly she fastens (O how quick˙ is love!);	*full of life*
39	The steed is stallèd up, and even now,	
40	To tie the rider she begins to prove.˙	*test*
41	Backward she push'd him, as she would˙ be thrust,	*wanted to*
42	And govern'd him in strength, though not in lust.	
43	So soon was she along˙ as he was down,	*lying by his side*
44	Each leaning on their elbows and their hips.	
45	Now doth she stroke his cheek, now doth he frown,	
46	And 'gins to chide, but soon she stops his lips,	
47	And kissing speaks, with lustful language broken,˙	*interrupted*
48	"If thou wilt chide, thy lips shall never open."	
49	He burns with bashful shame; she with her tears	
50	Doth quench the maiden˙ burning of his cheeks;	*virgin*
51	Then with her windy sighs, and golden hairs,	
52	To fan and blow them dry again she seeks.	
53	He saith she is immodest, blames her miss˙;	*immodesty*
54	What follows more, she murders with a kiss.	
55	Even as an empty eagle, sharp˙ by fast,˙	*eager for prey; fasting*
56	Tires˙ with her beak on feathers, flesh, and bone,	*tears ravenously*
57	Shaking her wings, devouring all in haste,	
58	Till either gorge˙ be stuff'd, or prey be gone;	*stomach*
59	Even so˙ she kiss'd his brow, his cheek, his chin,	*in this way*
60	And where she ends, she doth anew begin.	
61	Forc'd to content,˙ but never to obey,	*submit to her*
62	Panting he lies, and breatheth in her face.	
63	She feedeth on the steam, as on a prey,	
64	And calls it heavenly moisture, air of grace,	
65	Wishing her cheeks were gardens full of flowers,	
66	So they were˙ dew'd with such distilling showers.	*would be*

	67	Look˙ how a bird lies tangled in a net —
		just as
	68	So fasten'd in her arms Adonis lies;
	69	Pure shame and aw'd˙ resistance made him fret,
		daunted
	70	Which bred more beauty in his angry eyes:
The metaphor is of	71	Rain added to a river that is rank˙
tears in Adonis's eyes.		*luxuriously full*
	72	Perforce will force it overflow the bank.

67 Look˙ how a bird lies tangled in a net — *just as*
68 So fasten'd in her arms Adonis lies;
69 Pure shame and aw'd˙ resistance made him fret, *daunted*
70 Which bred more beauty in his angry eyes:
71   Rain added to a river that is rank˙ *luxuriously full*
72   Perforce will force it overflow the bank.

The metaphor is of tears in Adonis's eyes.

73 Still she entreats, and prettily entreats,
74 For to a pretty ear she tunes her tale.
75 Still is he sullen, still he lours and frets,
76 'Twixt crimson shame and anger ashy-pale.
77   Being˙ red, she loves him best; and being white, *he being*
78   Her best is better'd with a more delight.

79 Look how˙ he can, she cannot choose but love, *however*
80 And by her fair immortal hand she swears
81 From his soft bosom never to remove,˙ *remove herself*
82 Till he take truce with her contending tears,
83   Which long have rain'd, making her cheeks all wet,
84   And one sweet kiss shall pay this comptless˙ debt. *uncountable*

85 Upon this promise did he raise his chin,
86 Like a dive-dapper˙ peering through a wave, *waterbird*
87 Who being look'd on, ducks as quickly in.
88 So offers he to give what she did crave,
89   But when her lips were ready for his pay,˙ *payment of a kiss*
90   He winks,˙ and turns his lips another way. *shuts his eyes*

91 Never did passenger˙ in summer's heat *a traveler*
92 More thirst for drink, than she for this good turn.˙ *kiss*
93 Her help she sees, but help she cannot get;
94 She bathes in water,˙ yet her fire must burn. *tears*
95   "O pity," 'gan she cry, "flint-hearted boy,
96   'Tis but a kiss I beg; why art thou coy?

97 "I have been woo'd, as I entreat thee now,
*The **God of War** is Mars* 98 Even by the stern and direful God of War,
(in Greece called Ares). 99 Whose sinewy neck in battle ne'er did bow,
100 Who conquers where he comes in every jar˙; *fight*
101   Yet hath he been my captive, and my slave,
102   And begg'd for that which thou unask'd shalt have.

103 "Over my altars hath he˙ hung his lance,   *Mars*
104   His batter'd shield, his uncontrollèd˙ crest,˙   *unconquered; helmet*
105   And for my sake hath learn'd to sport, and dance,
106   To toy, to wanton, dally, smile, and jest,
107   Scorning his churlish˙ drum and ensign˙ red,   *violent; military flag*
108   Making my arms his field,˙ his tent my bed.   *battlefield*

109 "Thus he that over-rul'd, I over-sway'd,
110   Leading him prisoner in a red-rose˙ chain;   *flower*
111   Strong-temper'd steel his stronger strength obey'd,
112   Yet was he servile to my coy˙ disdain.   *teasing*
113   O, be not proud, nor brag not of thy might,
114   For mastering her that foil'd the God of fight.

115 "Touch˙ but my lips with those fair lips of thine—   *if you touch*
116   Though mine be not so fair, yet are they red—
117   The kiss shall be thine own, as well as mine.
118   What seest thou in the ground? Hold up thy head,
119   Look in mine eyeballs, there thy beauty lies;
120   Then why not lips on lips, since eyes in eyes?

121 "Art thou asham'd to kiss? Then wink˙ again,   *close your eyes*
122   And I will wink, so˙ shall the day seem night.   *in this way*
123   Love keeps his revels where there are but twain˙;   *two*
124   Be bold to play, our sport is not in sight˙;   *sight of anyone*
125   These blue-vein'd violets whereon we lean
126   Never can blab, nor know not what we mean.˙   *intend*

127 "The tender spring˙ upon thy tempting lip   *growth of hair (sprig of grass)*
128   Shows thee unripe,˙ yet may'st thou well be tasted.   *so young*
129   Make use of time, let not advantage slip,
130   Beauty within it self should not be wasted.
131   Fair flowers that are not gather'd in their prime,
132   Rot and consume themselves in little time.

This tells us Adonis is too young to grow a beard.

133 "Were I hard-favor'd,˙ foul, or wrinkled old,   *ugly*
134   Ill-nurtur'd, crooked, churlish, harsh in voice,
135   O'er-worn,˙ despisèd, rheùmatic, and cold,   *worn out by time*
136   Thick-sighted, barren, lean, and lacking juice,
137   Then mightst thou pause, for then I were not for thee,
138   But having no defècts, why dost abhor me?

139 "Thou canst not see one wrinkle in my brow;
140 Mine eyes are grey,˙ and bright, and quick in turning;   *blue*
141 My beauty, as the spring, doth yearly grow˙;   *renew itself*
142 My flesh is soft and plump, my marrow˙ burning;   *vital spirit*
143 My smooth moist hand, were it with thy hand felt,
144 Would in thy palm dissolve, or seem to melt.

145 "Bid me discourse, I will enchant thine ear;
146 Or like a fairy, trip˙ upon the green;   *dance*
147 Or like a nymph, with long dishevel'd hair,
148 Dance on the sands, and yet no footing˙ seen.   *footprint*
149 Love is a spirit all compàct˙ of fire,   *composed*
150 Not gross to sink, but light, and will aspire.˙   *rise*

151 "Witness this primrose bank whereon I lie,
152 These forceless˙ flowers like sturdy trees support me;   *weak*
153 Two strengthless doves will draw me˙ through the sky,   *my chariot*
154 From morn till night, even where I list˙ to sport me.   *choose*
155 Is love so light, sweet boy, and may it be
156 That thou should think it heavy unto thee?

157 "Is thine own heart to thine own face affected˙?   *in love*
158 Can thy right hand seize love upon˙ thy left?   *by clasping*
159 Then woo thy self, be of thy self rejected;
160 Steal thine own freedom, and complain on theft.

*Narcissus, Ovid tells us, was so beautiful everyone fell in love with him, but he wasn't interested in love until he saw **himself** reflected in a pool of water. He fell in love with **himself** and wasted away, staring at **himself**.*

161 Narcissus so˙ himself himself forsook,   *in this way*
162 And died to kiss his shadow in the brook.

163 "Torches are made to light, jewels to wear,
164 Dainties to taste, fresh beauty for the use,˙   *enjoyment*
165 Herbs for their smell, and sappy plants to bear˙;   *bear fruit*
166 Things growing to˙ themselves, are growth's abuse.   *only for*
167 Seeds spring from seeds, and beauty breedeth beauty:
168 Thou wast begot, to get˙ it is thy duty.   *beget beautiful children*

169 "Upon the earth's increase, why shouldst thou feed,
170 Unless the Earth with thy increase be fed?

This idea of the obligation to carry on one's beauty by having children is the theme of Shakespeare's Sonnets 1-17.

171 By law of Nature thou art bound to breed,
172 That thine˙ may live, when thou thy self art dead: *your offspring*
173 And so, in spite of death, thou dost survive,
174 In that thy likeness still is left alive.˙"   *alive in your children*

	175	By this˙ the love-sick Queen began to sweat,	*this time*
	176	For where they lay the shadow had forsook them,	
Titan here refers to	177	And Titan, tirèd in the mid-day heat,	
Sol, the Sun God	178	With burning eye did hotly over-look˙ them,	*survey*
(Helios in Greece).	179	Wishing Adonis had his˙ team˙ to guide,	*Titan's; team of horses*
It is now **mid-day.**	180	So he˙ were like him,˙ and by Venus' side.	*Titan; Adonis*

	181	And now Adonis, with a lazy sprite,˙	*spirit*
	182	And with a heavy, dark, disliking eye,	
	183	His louring brows o'er-whelming his fair sight,˙	*eyes*
	184	Like misty vapors when they blot the sky,	
	185	Souring˙ his cheeks, cries, "Fie, no more of love;	*anger coloring*
	186	The Sun doth burn my face—I must remove.˙"	*remove myself*

	187	"Ay, me," quoth Venus, "young, and so unkind˙?	*unnatural & unrelenting*
	188	What bare excuses mak'st thou to be gone?	
	189	I'll sigh celestial˙ breath, whose gentle wind	*godlike*
The **sun** *is now*	190	Shall cool the heat of this descending sun:	
descending.	191	I'll make a shadow for thee of my hairs;	
	192	If they burn too, I'll quench them with my tears.	

	193	"The Sun that shines from heaven, shines but warm,	
	194	And lo, I lie between that Sun, and thee:	
	195	The heat I have from thence˙ doth little harm—	*the Sun*
	196	Thine eye darts forth the fire that burneth me.	
	197	And were I not immortal, life were done˙	*destroyed*
The **earthly sun**	198	Between this heavenly and earthly sun.	
is Adonis.			

	199	"Art thou obdùrate, flinty, hard as steel?	
	200	Nay, more than flint, for stone at rain relenteth.˙	*erodes*
	201	Art thou a woman's son and canst not feel	
	202	What 'tis to love, how want˙ of love tormenteth?	*lack*
	203	O, had thy mother borne so hard a mind,	
She **died unkind,**	204	She had not brought forth thee, but died unkind.	
unnaturally, as not of			
her own kind, since	205	"What am I, that thou shouldst contemn˙ me thus?	*scorn*
womankind naturally	206	Or what great danger dwells upon my suit˙?	*plea*
have babies.	207	What, were thy lips the worse for one poor kiss?	
	208	Speak, fair,˙ but speak fair words, or else be mute.	*beautiful one*
	209	Give me one kiss; I'll give it thee again,	
	210	And one for int'rest, if thou wilt have twain.˙	*two*

211 "Fie, liveless picture; cold, and senseless stone;
212 Well-painted idol, image˙ dull and dead;   *painting*
213 Statue contenting but the eye alone,
214 Thing *like* a man, but of no woman bred:
215   Thou art no man, though of a man's complexion,˙   *appearance*
216   For men will kiss even by their own direction.˙"   *inclination*

217 This said, impatience chokes her pleading tongue,
218 And swelling passion doth provoke a pause.
219 Red cheeks and fiery eyes blaze forth her wrong;
220 Being judge in love, she cannot right her cause.
221   And now she weeps, and now she fain˙ would speak,   *gladly*
222   And now her sobs do her intendments break.˙   *interrupt*

223 Sometime she shakes her head, and then his hand;
224 Now gazeth she on him, now on the ground;
225 Sometime her arms enfold him like a band:
226 She would, he will not in her arms be bound.
227   And when from thence˙ he struggles to be gone,   *that place*
228   She locks her lily fingers one in one.

229 "Fondling," she saith, "since I have hemm'd thee here
230 Within the circuit of this ivory pale,˙   *fence (her fingers)*
231 I'll be a park,˙ and thou shalt be my deer: *deer preserve*
232 Feed where thou wilt, on mountain or in dale;
233   Graze on my lips, and if those hills be dry,
234   Stray lower, where the pleasant fountains lie.

235 "Within this limit˙ is relief˙ enough,   *boundary; pasture*
236 Sweet bottom grass, and high delightful plain,
237 Round rising hillocks, brakes˙ obscure and rough,   *thickets*
238 To shelter thee from tempest, and from rain.
239   Then be my deer, since I am such a park;
240   No dog shall rouse˙ thee, though a thousand bark."   *oust*

241 At this Adonis smiles as in disdain,
242 That˙ in each cheek appears a pretty dimple: *so that*
243 Love˙ made those hollows, if˙ himself were slain,   *Cupid; so that if*
244 He might be buried in a tomb so simple,˙   *plain & unadorned*
245   Foreknowing well, if there˙ he came to lie,   *in Adonis's dimples*
246   Why, there Love liv'd, and there he˙ could not die.   *Love/Cupid*

	247	These lovely caves,˙ these round enchanting pits,	*dimples*
*The **dimples** are so adorable that they swallow **Venus's** love.*	248	Open'd their mouths to swallow Venus' liking.	
	249	Being mad˙ before, how doth she now for wits?	*insane with love*
	250	Struck dead at first, what needs a second striking?	
	251	Poor Queen of Love, in thine own law˙ forlorn,	*sphere of influence*
	252	To love a cheek that smiles at thee in scorn.	

253 Now which way shall she turn? What shall she say?
254 Her words are done, her woes the more increasing;
255 The time is spent, her object will away,
256 And from her twining arms doth urge releasing:
257 "Pity," she cries, "some favor, some remorse.˙" — *compassion*
258 Away he springs, and hasteth to his horse.

*Here follows a lengthy and blatant metaphor of mating **horses**.*

259 But lo, from forth a copse˙ that neighbors by, — *patch of trees*
260 A breeding jennet,˙ lusty, young, and proud, — *Spanish mare*
261 Adonis' trampling courser˙ doth espy. — *stallion*
262 And forth she rushes, snorts, and neighs aloud.
263 The strong-neck'd steed, being tied unto a tree,
264 Breaketh his rein, and to her straight goes he.

The horse breaks all bonds so to have uncontrolled sex.

265 Imperiously he leaps, he neighs, he bounds,
266 And now his woven girths˙ he breaks asunder; — *belt cloths*
267 The bearing Earth with his hard hoof he wounds,
268 Whose hollow womb resounds like heaven's thunder.
269 The iron bit he crusheth 'tween his teeth,
270 Controlling what he was controllèd with.

271 His ears up-prick'd, his braided hanging mane
272 Upon his compass'd˙ crest now stand on end; — *rounded*
273 His nostrils drink the air, and forth again
274 As from a furnace, vapors doth he send;
275 His eye, which scornfully glisters like fire,
276 Shows his hot courage,˙ and his high desire. — *lust*

277 Sometime he trots, as if he told˙ the steps, — *numbered*
278 With gentle majesty and modest pride;
279 Anon he rears upright, curvets,˙ and leaps, — *hops on back legs*
280 As who should say, "Lo, thus my strength is tried,˙ — *tested*
281 And this I do, to captivate the eye
282 Of the fair breeder that is standing by."

283	What recketh˙ he his rider's angry stir,	*cares*
284	His flattering, "Holla," or his, "Stand, I say"?	
285	What cares he now, for curb, or pricking spur,	
286	For rich caparisons,˙ or trappings gay?	*ornamental coverings*
287	He sees his love, and nothing else he sees,	
288	For nothing else with his proud sight agrees.	

289	Look˙ when a painter would surpass the life,	*just like*
290	In limning˙ out a well-proportion'd steed,	*painting*
291	His Art with Nature's workmanship at strife,	
292	As if the dead˙ the living should exceed;	*inanimate*
293	So˙ did this horse excel a common one,	*in the same way*
294	In shape, in courage, color, pace, and bone.˙	*frame*

*As if the painted image **should exceed the living** creature.*

295	Round hoof'd, short-jointed, fetlocks shag˙ and long,	*shaggy*
296	Broad breast, full eye, small head, and nostril wide,	
297	High crest,˙ short ears, straight legs, and passing strong,	*neck ridge*
298	Thin mane, thick tail, broad buttock, tender hide:	
299	Look what˙ a horse should have, he did not lack,	*whatever*
300	Save˙ a proud rider on so proud a back.	*except*

301	Sometime he scuds˙ far off, and there he stares,	*rushes*
302	Anon he starts˙ at stirring of a feather;	*startles*
303	To bid the wind a base,˙ he now prepares,	*running game*
304	And whe'er he run, or fly, they know not whether,˙	*whether he runs or flies*
305	For through his mane and tail, the high wind sings,	
306	Fanning the hairs, who wave like feather'd wings.	

307	He looks upon his love, and neighs unto her;	
308	She answers him, as if she knew his mind.	
309	Being proud, as females are, to see him woo her,	
310	She puts on outward strangeness,˙ seems unkind,	*indifference*
311	Spurns˙ at his love, and scorns the heat he feels,	*kicks*
312	Beating his kind˙ embracements with her heels.	*natural*

313	Then, like a melancholy malcontent,	
314	He vails˙ his tail that, like a falling plume,	*lowers*
315	Cool shadow to his melting buttock lent;	
316	He stamps, and bites the poor flies in his fume.˙	*anger*
317	His love,˙ perceiving how he was enrag'd,	*(the mare)*
318	Grew kinder, and his fury was assuag'd.	

His testy Master, *of course, is Adonis.*	319	His testy Master˙ goeth about to take him,	
	320	When lo, the unback'd˙ breeder,˙ full of fear,	*riderless; mare*
	321	Jealous˙ of catching, swiftly doth forsake him;	*suspicious*
	322	With her the horse,˙ and left Adonis there:	*stallion*
	323	As˙ they were mad, unto the wood they hie them,	*as if*
	324	Outstripping crows that strive to over-fly them.	

We leave the horse metaphor.

325 All swoll'n with chafing,˙ down Adonis sits,   *anger*
326 Banning˙ his boist'rous and unruly beast;   *cursing*
327 And now the happy˙ season once more fits   *fortuitous*
328 That love-sick Love, by pleading, may be bless'd;
329 For lovers say, the heart hath treble wrong
330 When it is barr'd the aidance˙ of the tongue.   *assistance*

331 An oven that is stopp'd,˙ or river stay'd,˙   *stopped up; dammed*
332 Burneth more hotly, swelleth with more rage;
333 So˙ of concealèd sorrow may be said.   *the same*
334 Free vent˙ of words love's fire doth assuage,   *outpouring*

The heart's attorney *is the tongue.*

335 But when the heart's attorney once is mute,
336 The client˙ breaks, as desperate in his suit.   *heart*

337 He˙ sees her˙ coming, and begins to glow,   *Adonis; Venus*
338 Even as a dying coal revives with wind,

*Adonis wears a **bonnet** or hat in only one version of the painting by Titian, which is on the cover of this book.*

339 And with his bonnet hides his angry brow,
340 Looks on the dull earth with disturbèd mind,
341 Taking no notice that she is so nigh,
342 For all askance˙ he holds her in his eye.   *sideways & suspiciously*

343 O, what a sight it was, wistly˙ to view,   *earnestly*
344 How she came stealing to the wayward boy,
345 To note the fighting conflict of her hue,
346 How white and red, each other did destroy:
347 But now˙ her cheek was pale, and by and by   *recently*
348 It flash'd forth fire, as lightning from the sky.

349 Now was she just before him as he sat,
350 And like a lowly lover, down she kneels;
351 With one fair hand she heaveth up his hat,
352 Her other tender hand his fair cheek feels:
353 His tenderer cheek receives her soft hand's print,
354 As apt˙ as new-fall'n snow takes any dint.˙   *readily; impression*

355	O what a war of looks was then between them:	
356	Her eyes, petitioners˙ to his eyes suing,˙	*beggars; begging*
357	His eyes saw her eyes, as˙ they had not seen them;	*as if*
358	Her eyes woo'd still, his eyes disdain'd the wooing:	
359	And all this dumb˙ play had his acts made plain	*silent*
360	With tears which, chorus-like, her eyes did rain.	

*A **dumb play,** or dumb show (as in **Hamlet**), is a performance without words. Venus's **tears** act as a **chorus** to interpret the action.*

361	Full gently now she takes him by the hand,	
362	A lily prison'd in a jail of snow,	
363	Or ivory in an alabaster band˙;	*bond*
364	So white a friend engirts˙ so white a foe.	*surrounds*
365	This beauteous combat, willful and unwilling,	
366	Show'd like two silver doves that sit a-billing.	

*Here **the engine** is her tongue.*

367	Once more the engine of her thoughts began:	
368	"O fairest mover on this mortal round,˙	*Earth*
369	Would˙ thou wert as I am, and I a man,	*I wish*
370	My heart all whole as thine, thy heart my˙ wound.	*feeling my*
371	For one sweet look, thy help I would assure thee,	
372	Though nothing but my body's bane˙ would cure thee."	*ruin*
373	"Give me my hand," saith he, "why dost thou feel˙ it?"	*hang on to*
374	"Give me my heart," saith she, "and thou shalt have it.˙	*your hand*
375	O give it me, lest thy hard heart do steel˙ it,	*harden*
376	And being steel'd, soft sighs can never grave˙ it.	*engrave on*
377	Then love's deep groans I never shall regard,	
378	Because Adonis' heart hath made mine hard."
379	"For shame," he cries, "let go, and let me go;	
380	My day's delight is past, my horse is gone,	
381	And 'tis your fault I am bereft˙ him so.	*deprived of*
382	I pray you, hence,˙ and leave me here alone,	*go away*
383	For all my mind, my thought, my busy care,	
384	Is how to get my palfrey˙ from the mare."	*saddle horse*
385	Thus she replies, "Thy palfrey, as he should,	
386	Welcomes the warm approach of sweet desire;	
387	Affection˙ is a coal that must be cool'd,	*passion*
388	Else suffer'd,˙ it will set the heart on fire.	*allowed to burn*
389	The sea hath bounds, but deep desire hath none;	
390	Therefore no marvel though thy horse be gone.	

391 "How like a jade˙ he˙ stood, tied to the tree,   *broken-down nag; the stallion*
392   Servilely master'd with a leathern rein;
393   But when he saw his love, his youth's fair fee,˙   *reward*
394   He held such petty bondage in disdain,
395   Throwing the base thong from his bending crest,˙   *neck*
396   Enfranchising˙ his mouth, his back, his breast.   *freeing*

*Elizabethans did not wear any clothing to bed, thus it is a **naked bed**.*

397 "Who sees his true-love in her naked bed,
398   Teaching the sheets a whiter hue than white,
399   But˙ when his glutton eye so full hath fed,   *but that*
400   His other agents˙ aim at like˙ delight?   *senses; similar*
401   Who is so faint that dares not be so bold
402   To touch the fire, the weather being cold?

403 "Let me excuse thy courser,˙ gentle boy,   *horse*
404   And learn of him, I heartily beseech thee,
405   To take advantage on presented joy.
406   Though I were dumb,˙ yet his proceedings teach thee.   *unable to speak*
407   O learn to love, the lesson is but plain,
408   And once made perfect,˙ never lost again."   *perfectly by heart*

409 "I know not love," quoth he, "nor will not know it,
410   Unless it be a boar, and then I chase it;
411   'Tis much to borrow, and I will not owe it.
412   My love to love, is love but˙ to disgrace˙ it,   *only; discredit*
413   For I have heard, it is a life in death,
414   That laughs and weeps, and all but with a˙ breath.   *one*

415 "Who wears a garment shapeless and unfinish'd?
416   Who plucks the bud before one leaf put forth?
417   If springing˙ things be any jot diminish'd,   *sprouting & immature*
418   They wither in their prime, prove nothing worth.
419   The colt that's back'd˙ and burden'd,˙ being young,   *broken in; ridden*
420   Loseth his pride, and never waxeth strong.

421 "You hurt my hand with wringing; let us part,
422   And leave this idle theme, this bootless˙ chat.   *useless*
423   Remove your siege from my unyielding heart,
424   To love's alarms˙ it will not ope the gate.   *attacks*
425   Dismiss your vows, your feignèd tears, your flatt'ry,
426   For where a heart is hard, they make no batt'ry."˙   *hole in a wall*

427 "What, canst thou talk," quoth she, "hast thou a tongue?

428 O, would˙ thou hadst not, or I had no hearing.   *I wish*

429 Thy mermaid's˙ voice hath done me double wrong;   *siren's*

430 I had my load˙ before, now press'd with bearing: *burden of desire*

431   Melodious discord, heavenly tune harsh-sounding,

432   Ears' deep sweet music, and heart's deep sore-wounding.

433 "Had I no eyes but ears, my ears would love

434 That inward beauty and invisible˙;   *(his voice)*

435 Or were I˙ deaf, thy outward parts would move   *I also*

436 Each part in me that were but sensible.

437   Though neither eyes nor ears, to hear nor see,

438   Yet should I be in love, by *touching* thee.

*Creatures with five **senses** (touch, taste, sight, smell, hearing, all of which are mentioned in lines 433–445), are **sensible.** Rocks, for instance, are not **sensible.***

439 "Say that the sense of feeling were˙ bereft me,   *were also*

440 And that I could not see, nor hear, nor touch,

441 And nothing but the very smell were left me,

442 Yet would my love to thee be still as much;

443   For from the stillitory˙ of thy face excelling,   *distillation*

444   Comes breath perfum'd, that breedeth love by smelling.

*Adonis is the **banquet.***

445 "But oh, what banquet wert thou to the taste,

446 Being nurse and feeder of the other four.˙   *four senses*

447 Would they not wish the feast might ever-last,

448 And bid Suspicion˙ double-lock the door,   *caution*

449   Lest Jealousy, that sour unwelcome guest,

450   Should, by his stealing in, disturb the feast?"

451 Once more the ruby-color'd portal˙ open'd,   *doorway (mouth)*

452 Which to his speech did honey passage yield,

453 Like a red morn, that ever yet betoken'd

*"Red sky at night, sailor's delight; **Red** sky at **morning,** sailors take warning."*

454 Wrack˙ to the sea-man, tempest to the field,˙   *shipwreck; grain*

455   Sorrow to shepherds, woe unto the birds,

456   Gusts and foul flaws˙ to herdmen, and to herds.   *blasts of wind*

457 This ill presàge˙ advisedly she marketh: *omen*

458 Even as the wind is hush'd before it raineth,

459 Or as the wolf doth grin˙ before he barketh,   *bare its teeth*

460 Or as the berry breaks before it staineth,

461   Or like the deadly bullet of a gun,

462   His meaning struck her ere˙ his words begun.   *before*

	463	And at his look, she flatly falleth down,
	464	For looks kill love, and love by looks reviveth;
	465	A smile recures˙ the wounding of a frown.	*heals*

*She feigns **bankruptcy** of love, but by this she **thrives** in that she gets a fortune, to her, in Adonis's attention.*

466	But blessèd bankrupt that by love so thriveth—	
467	The silly˙ boy, believing she is dead,	*naive*
468	Claps her pale cheek, till clapping makes it red;	

469	And all amaz'd, brake˙ off his late˙ intent,	*broke; recent*
470	For sharply he did think to reprehend˙ her,	*scold*
471	Which cunning Love did wittily prevent.	
472	Fair-fall˙ the wit that can so well defend her:	*good luck befall*
473	For on the grass she lies as˙ she were slain,	*as though*
474	Till his breath breatheth˙ life in her again.	*were to breathe*

*Apparently **wringing** (stopping) the **nose** briefly was used to induce a person to breathe again.*

475	He wrings her nose, he strikes her on the cheeks,	
476	He bends her fingers, holds her pulses hard,	
477	He chafes her lips, a thousand ways he seeks	
478	To mend the hurt that his unkindness marr'd.˙	*caused harm*
479	He kisses her, and she, by her good will,˙	*intention*
480	Will never rise, so˙ he will kiss her still.˙	*so that; forever*

481	The night of sorrow now is turn'd to day:	
482	Her two blue windows˙ faintly she upheaveth,	*eyes*
483	Like the fair Sun, when in his˙ fresh array	*its*
484	He cheers the Morn, and all the Earth relieveth˙;	*is relieved*

*In the same way that the **Sun glorifies the sky**, her own face is **illumined** with the sight of Adonis.*

485	And as the bright Sun glorifies the sky,	
486	So is her face illumin'd with her eye,˙	*eyes' sight of Adonis*

487	Whose beams˙ upon his hairless face are fix'd,	*eye beams*
488	As if from thence˙ they borrow'd all their shine.	*that place*
489	Were never four such lamps˙ together mix'd,	*eyes*
490	Had not his˙ clouded with his brow's repine.˙	*his eyes; annoyance*
491	But hers, which through the crystal tears gave light,	
492	Shone like the Moon in water seen by night.	

493	"O, where am I," quoth she, "in earth or heaven,	
494	Or in the ocean drench'd, or in the fire?	
495	What hour is this, or morn, or weary even˙;	*evening*
496	Do I delight to die, or life desire?	

*Life was as **annoying** and wearisome as **death**; **death was joyful** as **life**, because when Adonis thought she was dead, he paid attention to her.*

497	But˙ now I liv'd, and life was death's annoy,	*just*
498	But˙ now I died, and death was lively joy.	*just*

499 "O, *thou* didst kill me—kill me once again;

500 Thy eyes' shrewd˙ tutor, that hard heart of thine,   *scheming*

501 Hath taught them˙ scornful tricks, and such disdain   *your eyes*

502 That they have murder'd this poor heart of mine,

503   And these mine eyes, true leaders to their Queen,

504   But˙ for thy piteous lips, no more had seen.   *were it not*

*Her **eyes'** Queen is her heart.* (lines 503–504)

505 "Long may they˙ kiss each other, for this cure;   *your lips*

506 Oh, never let their crimson liveries˙ wear.˙   *uniforms; wear out*

507 And as they last, their verdure˙ still endure,   *medicinal herbal qualities*

508 To drive infection from the dangerous year,

509   That the star-gazers,˙ having writ˙ on death,   *astrologers; predicted*

510   May say, the plague is banish'd by thy breath.

*A **seal** makes an **imprint** in hot **wax,** used to sign **bargains** or contracts.* (lines 511–516)

511 "Pure lips, sweet seals in my soft lips imprinted,

512 What bargains may I make, still˙ to be sealing˙?   *always; kissing*

513 To sell my self, I can be well contented,

514 So˙ thou wilt buy, and pay, and use good dealing,   *as long as*

515   Which purchase if thou make, for fear of slips,˙   *errors*

516   Set thy seal manual on my wax-red lips.

517 "A thousand kisses buys my heart from me,

518 And pay them at thy leisure, one by one.

519 What is ten hundred touches˙ unto thee—   *kisses*

520 Are they not quickly told,˙ and quickly gone?   *counted*

521   Say for non-payment, that the debt should double,

522   Is twenty hundred kisses such a trouble?"

523 "Fair Queen," quoth he, "if any love you owe˙ me,   *carry for*

524 Measure my strangeness˙ with my unripe years: *shyness*

525 Before I know my self, seek not to know me—

526 No fisher but the ungrown fry forbears.˙   *refrains from*

527   The mellow plum doth fall; the green sticks fast,

528   Or being early pluck'd, is sour to taste.

*There are **no fisher**men who don't throw back **the fry,** the fish that are too young.* (lines 526–528)

529 "Look, the world's comforter, with weary gait,

530 His day's hot task hath ended in the West;

531 The owl (Night's herald) shrieks; 'tis very late;

532 The sheep are gone to fold, birds to their nest,

533   And coal-black clouds, that shadow heaven's light,˙   *(the Moon)*

534   Do summon us to part, and bid good night.

*The **world's comforter** is the Sun.* (lines 529–530)

*The **owl** is also an omen of death.* (line 531)

*Now it is **night**-time; the poem started in the early morn.* (line 534)

535 "Now let me say good night, and so say you;
536   If you will say so, you shall have a kiss."
537 "Good night," quoth she, and ere he says adieu,
538 The honey-fee of parting tender'd˙ is.   *given*
539   Her arms do lend his neck a sweet embrace;
540   Incorporate˙ then they seem, face grows to face.   *one body*

541 Till, breathless, he disjoin'd, and backward drew
542 The heavenly moisture, that sweet coral mouth,
543 Whose precious taste her thirsty lips well knew,
544 Whereon they surfeit,˙ yet complain on drought;   *indulge to excess*
545   He with her plenty press'd,˙ she faint with dearth,˙   *oppressed; scarcity*
546   Their lips together glued, fall to the earth.

547 Now quick desire hath caught the yielding prey,
548 And glutton-like she feeds, yet never filleth.
549 Her lips are conquerors; his lips obey,
550 Paying what ransom the insulter˙ willeth,   *bragging conqueror*
551   Whose vulture˙ thought doth pitch the price so high   *ravenous*
552   That she will draw his lips' rich treasure dry.

553 And having felt the sweetness of the spoil,˙   *booty she plundered*
554 With blind-fold fury she begins to forage˙:   *ravage him*
555 Her face doth reek˙ and smoke, her blood doth boil,   *steam*
556 And careless Lust stirs up a desperate courage,
557   Planting˙ Oblivion, beating Reason back,   *causing*
558   Forgetting Shame's pure blush, and Honor's wrack.˙   *ruin*

559 Hot, faint, and weary with her hard embracing,
560 Like a wild bird being tam'd with too much handling,
561 Or as the fleet-foot roe˙ that's tir'd with chasing,   *small deer*
562 Or like the froward˙ infant still'd with dandling: *cantankerous*
563   He now obeys, and now no more resisteth,
564   While she takes all she can, not all she listeth.˙   *desire*

565 What wax so frozen but dissolves with temp'ring,˙   *heating & handling*
566 And yields at last to every light impression?
567 Things out of hope are compass'd˙ oft with vent'ring,˙   *achieved; risking*
568 Chiefly in love, whose leave˙ exceeds commission.˙   *liberty; authority*
569   Affection˙ faints not like a pale-fac'd coward,   *passion*
570   But then woos best, when most his choice is froward.˙   *perverse*

*Affection woos best when the object of love, Affection's **choice**, does not give in.*

571	When he did frown, O had she then gave over,	
572	Such nectar from his lips she had not suck'd.	
573	Foul words, and frowns, must not repel a lover;	
574	What though the rose have prickles, yet˙ 'tis pluck'd.	*still*
575	Were beauty under twenty locks kept fast,	
576	Yet love breaks through, and picks them all at last.	

Picking a lock can have sexual connotations.

577	For pity˙ now she can no more detain him;	*appealing to his pity*
578	The poor fool prays˙ her that he may depart.	*begs*
579	She is resolv'd no longer to restrain him,	
580	Bids him farewell, and look˙ well to her heart,	*take care*
581	The which, by Cupid's bow she doth protest,˙	*avow*
582	He carries thence˙ encagèd in his breast.	*away from there*

583	"Sweet boy," she says, "this night I'll waste˙ in sorrow,	*spend*
584	For my sick heart commands mine eyes to watch.˙	*stay awake*
585	Tell me, Love's master, shall we meet to-morrow?	
586	Say, shall we, shall we, wilt thou make the match?"	
587	He tells her no, to-morrow he intends	
588	To hunt the boar with certain of his friends.	

589	"The boar," quoth she, whereat a sudden pale,˙	*pallor*
590	Like lawn˙ being spread upon the blushing rose,	*fine linen*
591	Usurps˙ her cheek; she trembles at his tale,	*takes over*
592	And on his neck her yoking arms she throws.	
593	She sinketh down, still hanging by his neck;	
594	He on her belly falls, she on her back.	

595	Now is she in the very lists˙ of love,	*tournament arena*
596	Her champion mounted for the hot encounter;	
597	All is imaginary she˙ doth prove.˙	*that she; experience*
598	He will not manage˙ her, although he mount her,	*cope with*
599	That˙ worse than Tantalus' is her annoy,	*so that*
600	To clip˙ Elysium, and to lack her joy.	*embrace*

Tantalus has to stand in a pond beneath a fruit tree: the fruit is always out of reach, and the water always recedes when he tries to drink.

Elysium is paradise (only relatives of Gods and certain heroes can go there).

601	Even so˙ poor birds, deceiv'd with painted grapes,	*in this way*
602	Do surfeit by the eye and pine˙ the maw˙;	*starve; stomach*
603	Even so she languisheth in her mishaps,	
604	As˙ those poor birds that helpless˙ berries saw.	*like; useless*
605	The warm effects˙ which she in him finds missing,	*sexual response*
606	She seeks to kindle with continual kissing.	

Although none of the paintings of Zeuxis (4th century BCE) survive, Pliny tells of his **painting of grapes** that look so real **birds** try to eat them.

607	But all in vain, good Queen, it will not be;	
608	She hath assay'd˙ as much as may be prov'd.˙	*attempted; tried*
609	Her pleading˙ hath deserv'd a greater fee;	*legal appeal*
610	She's love, she loves, and yet she is not lov'd.	
611	"Fie, fie," he says, "you crush me, let me go;	
612	You have no reason to withhold me so."	

613	"Thou hadst been gone," quoth she, "sweet boy, ere˙ this,	*before*
614	But that thou toldst me thou wouldst hunt the boar.	
615	Oh, be advis'd, thou know'st not what it is	
616	With javelin's point a churlish˙ swine to gore,	*violent*
617	Whose tushes,˙ never sheath'd, he whetteth still,˙	*tusks; constantly*
618	Like to a mortal˙ butcher, bent to kill.	*deadly*

619	"On his bow-back,˙ he hath a battle set	*arched back*
620	Of bristly pikes, that ever˙ threat his foes;	*always*
621	His eyes like glow-worms shine when he doth fret˙;	*rage*
622	His snout digs sepulchers˙ wheresoe'er he goes;	*graves*
623	Being mov'd,˙ he strikes, what e'er is in his way,	*annoyed*
624	And whom he strikes, his crooked tushes slay.	

625	"His brawny sides, with hairy bristles armèd,	
626	Are better proof˙ than thy spear's point can enter;	*armor*
627	His short, thick neck cannot be easily harmèd;	
628	Being ireful, on the lion he will venture.˙	*risk an assault*
629	The thorny brambles and embracing bushes,	
630	As˙ fearful of him, part, through whom he rushes.	*as if*

631	"Alas, he naught esteems˙ that face of thine,	*respects*
632	To which Love's eyes pays tributary gazes,	
633	Nor thy soft hands, sweet lips, and crystal eyne,˙	*eyes*
634	Whose full perfection all the world amazes;	
635	But having thee at vantage˙ (wondrous dread!)	*a disadvantage*
636	Would root these beauties as he roots the mead.˙	*meadow*

637	"Oh, let him keep˙ his loathsome cabin˙ still;	*stay within; den*
638	Beauty hath naught to do with such foul fiends.	
639	Come not within his danger by thy will;	
640	They that thrive well, take counsel of their friends.	
641	When thou didst name the boar, not to dissemble,˙	*pretend*
642	I fear'd˙ thy fortune, and my joints did tremble.	*feared for*

643 "Didst thou not mark my face, was it not white?
644 Saw'st thou not signs of fear lurk in mine eye?
645 Grew I not faint, and fell I not down-right?
646 Within my bosom, whereon thou dost lie,
647   My boding˙ heart pants, beats, and takes no rest,   *foreboding*
648   But like an earthquake, shakes thee on my breast.

649 "For where Love reigns, disturbing Jealousy
650 Doth call himself 'Affection's Sentinel,'
651 Gives false alarms, suggesteth˙ mutiny,   *incites*
652 And in a peaceful hour doth cry, "Kill, kill,"
653   Distemp'ring˙ gentle Love in his desire,   *deranging the condition of*
654   As air and water do abate˙ the fire.   *extinguish*

655 "This sour informer, this bate˙-breeding spy,   *strife*
656 This canker˙ that eats up Love's tender spring,˙   *worm; blossom*
657 This carry-tale, dissentious˙ Jealousy,   *quarrelsome*
658 That sometime true news, sometime false, doth bring,
659   Knocks at my heart, and whispers in mine ear,
660   That if I love thee, I thy death should fear;

661 "And more than so, presenteth to mine eye
662 The picture of an angry, chafing boar,
663 Under whose sharp fangs, on his back doth lie
664 An image like thy self, all stain'd with gore,
665   Whose blood upon the fresh flowers being shed,
666   Doth make them droop with grief, and hang the head.

667 "What should I do, seeing thee so indeed,˙   *in reality*
668 That˙ tremble at th' imagination?   *when I*
669 The thought of it doth make my faint heart bleed,
670 And fear doth teach it divination.˙   *prophetic power*
671   I prophesy thy death, my living sorrow,
672   If thou encounter with the boar to-morrow.

673 "But if thou needs˙ wilt hunt, be rul'd by me: *insistently*
674 Uncouple˙ at the timorous flying hare;   *unleash the hounds*
675 Or at the fox, which lives by subtlety;
676 Or at the roe,˙ which no encounter dare.   *small deer*
677   Pursue these fearful˙ creatures o'er the downs,   *frightened*
678   And on thy well-breath'd˙ horse keep with thy hounds.   *strong*

Since line 594, he's been lying on top of her, held there by Venus.

***Jealousy** here seems to mean more than suspicion—it's more like an apprehension of evil; see line 660.*

Here is a foreshadow of Adonis's end.

	679	"And when thou hast on foot the purblind˙ hare,	*dim-sighted*
	680	Mark the poor wretch, to over-shoot˙ his troubles,	*run past*
	681	How he outruns the wind, and with what care	
He twists and turns *and **doubles** back.*	682	He cranks and crosses with a thousand doubles:	
	683	The many musets˙ through the which he goes,	*gaps in hedges*
	684	Are like a labyrinth t'amaze˙ his foes.	*befuddle*

685 "Sometime he runs among a flock of sheep,
686 To make the cunning hounds mistake their smell;
687 And sometime where earth-delving coneys˙ keep, — *rabbits*
688 To stop the loud pursuers in their yell;
689 And sometime sorteth˙ with a herd of deer. — *hangs out with*
690 Danger deviseth shifts,˙ wit waits˙ on fear. — *strategies; attends*

691 "For there his smell with others being minglèd,
692 The hot scent-snuffing hounds are driv'n to doubt,
693 Ceasing their clamorous cry, till they have singlèd,
694 With much ado, the cold fault˙ cleanly out. — *scent*
695 Then do they spend˙ their mouths; Echo replies, — *use*
696 As if an other chase were in the skies.

Zeus was "visiting"
lovely nymphs on Earth,
*as usual, and told **Echo**,*
(a nymph) to chatter with
Hera (his wife) to distract
her from his goings-on.
Hera saw through the ploy
*and cursed **Echo** with being*
able to repeat only the last
words someone else said.

697 "By this, poor Wat,˙ far off upon a hill, — *Wat the rabbit*
698 Stands on his hinder-legs with list'ning ear,
699 To hearken if his foes pursue him still.
700 Anon˙ their loud alarums he doth hear, — *soon*
701 And now his grief may be comparèd well,
702 To one sore sick, that˙ hears the passing bell. — *who*

***Bells** are tolled at*
funerals to keep away
the evil spirits.

703 "Then shalt thou see the dew-bedabbl'd wretch
704 Turn, and return, indenting˙ with the way; — *zig-zagging*
705 Each envious˙ briar his weary legs do scratch; — *spiteful*
706 Each shadow makes him stop, each murmur stay,
707 For misery˙ is trodden on by many, — *a miserable being*
708 And being low, never reliev'd by any.

709 "Lie quietly, and hear a little more;
710 Nay, do not struggle, for thou shalt not rise.
711 To make thee hate the hunting of the boar,

***Unlike my self**, as the*
Goddess of Love.

712 Unlike my self, thou hear'st me moralize,˙ — *lecture on behavior*
713 Applying this to that, and so to so,
714 For love can comment ùpon every woe.

*She means, "Where did I leave off my story?" But he responds with **leave me** as in **go away**.*	715	"Where did I leave?" "No matter where," quoth he,	
	716	"Leave *me,* and then the story aptly ends —	
	717	The night is spent." "Why, what of that?" quoth she.	
	718	"I am," quoth he, "expected of my friends,	
	719	And now 'tis dark, and going, I shall fall."	*while walking*
	720	"In night," quoth she, "desire sees best of all.	

"But if thou fall, oh then, imagine this:
721
722   The Earth, in love with thee, thy footing trips,
723   And all is but to rob thee of a kiss.
724   Rich preys make true men thieves: so do thy lips   *loot; honest*
725   Make modest Dìan cloudy and forlorn,
726   Lest she should steal a kiss and die forsworn.

*Dian (aka Diana, **Cynthia**), Goddess of the Moon, is an avowed virgin so if she **stole a kiss** from a man, that would be breaking her vow; she would be **forsworn**.*

727 "Now of this dark night I perceive the reason: *for*
728   Cynthia, for shame, obscures her silver shine,
729   Till forging Nature be condemn'd of treason   *counterfeiting*
730   For stealing molds from heaven that were divine,
731   Wherein she fram'd thee, in high heaven's despite,   *Nature*
732   To shame the Sun by day, and her by night.   *Cynthia*

*Nature created **thee**, Adonis, in **despite**, or in defiance, of **heaven**.*

733 "And therefore hath she brib'd the Destinies   *Cynthia*
734   To cross the curious workmanship of Nature,   *obstruct; ingenious*
735   To mingle beauty with infirmities,
736   And pure perfection with impure defeature,   *disfigurement*
737   Making it subject to the tyranny   *beauty*
738   Of mad mischances and much misery,   *calamities*

*An **ague** (EGG you) is an illness like the flu.*

739 "As burning fevers, agues pale and faint,   *such as*
740   Life-poisoning pestilence, and frenzies wood,   *lunatic*

*Love melts the **marrow**, the vital spirit, in our bones.*

741   The marrow-eating sickness whose attaint   *infection*
742   Disorder breeds by heating of the blood,
743   Surfeits, impostumes, grief, and damn'd despair   *abscesses*
744   Swear Nature's death, for framing thee so fair.   *because of*

745 "And not the least of all these maladies,
746   But in one minute's fight brings Beauty under.
747   Both favor, savor, hue, and qualities,   *beautiful features & form*
748   Whereat th' impartial gazer late did wonder,   *lately*
749   Are on the sudden wasted, thaw'd, and done,   *wasted away*
750   As mountain snow melts with the midday sun.

751 "Therefore, despite˙ of fruitless˙ chastity —   *in defiance; barren*

752   Love-lacking vestals˙ and self-loving nuns,   *vestal virgins*

753   That˙ on the Earth would breed a scarcity   *who*

754   And barren dearth of daughters, and of sons —

755   Be prodigal; the lamp˙ that burns by night   *moon*

756   Dries up his˙ oil to lend the world his˙ light.   *its; its*

Again, this is the argument of Sonnets 1-17, that a beautiful person is obligated to create children to carry on their beauty.

757 "What is thy body but a swallowing grave,

758   Seeming to bury that posterity˙   *future generation*

759   Which, by the rights of time, thou needs must have,

760   If thou destroy them not in dark obscurity?

761   If so, the world will hold thee in disdain,

762   Sith˙ in thy pride, so fair a hope is slain.   *since*

763 "So in thy self, thy self art made away,˙   *non-existent*

Civil home-bred strife *is civil war, a constant issue in Shakespeare's history plays.*

764   A mischief˙ worse than civil home-bred strife,   *evil*

765   Or theirs whose desperate hands themselves do slay,

766   Or butcher-sire that reaves˙ his son of life.   *robs*

767   Foul cank'ring˙ rust, the hidden treasure frets˙;   *consuming; eats away*

768   But gold that's put to use, more gold begets."

769 "Nay then," quoth Adon, "you will fall again,

770   Into your idle˙ over-handl'd theme.   *useless*

771   The kiss I gave you is bestow'd in vain,

772   And all in vain you strive against the stream,

*The darkness of **Night** **nurses,** or encourages, **foul desire.***

773   For by this black-fac'd Night, desire's foul nurse,

774   Your treatise˙ makes me like you worse and worse.   *discourse*

775 "If love have lent you twenty thousand tongues,

776   And every tongue more moving˙ than your own,   *persuasive*

777   Bewitching like the wanton mermaids' songs,

778   Yet˙ from˙ mine ear the tempting tune is blown;   *still; away from*

*Her **heart** is **armed** and on guard.*

779   For know, my heart stands armèd in mine ear,

780   And will not let a false sound enter there,

781 "Lest the deceiving harmony should run

782   Into the quiet closure˙ of my breast,   *enclosure*

783   And then my little heart were quite undone,

784   In his˙ bed-chamber to be barr'd of rest.   *my heart's own*

785   No, Lady, no, my heart longs not to groan,

786   But soundly sleeps, while now it sleeps alone.

787 "What have you urg'd, that I can not reprove˙?   *refute*
788 The path is smooth that leadeth on to danger.
789 I hate not love, but your device˙ in love,   *sly action*
790 That lends embracements unto every stranger.
791   You do it for "increase"—O, strange excuse,
792   When Reason is the bawd˙ to Lust's abuse.   *pimp*

793 "Call it not love, for Love to heaven is fled,
794 Since sweating Lust on earth usurp'd his˙ name,   *Love's*
795 Under whose˙ simple semblance he˙ hath fed   *Love's; Lust*
796 Upon fresh beauty, blotting it with blame,
797   Which the hot tyrant stains, and soon bereaves,˙   *spoils*
798   As caterpillars do the tender leaves.

799 "Love comforteth like sun-shine after rain,
800 But Lust's effect is tempest after sun;
801 Love's gentle spring doth always fresh remain,
802 Lust's winter comes ere summer half be done;
803   Love surfeits not, Lust like a glutton dies;
804   Love is all truth, Lust full of forgèd lies.

805 "More I could tell, but more I dare not say:
*Adonis is the **orator**.* 806 The text is old,˙ the orator too green,˙   *persistent; inexperienced*
807 Therefore, in sadness,˙ now I will away.   *all seriousness*
808 My face is full of shame; my heart of teen˙;   *vexation*
809   Mine ears, that to your wanton˙ talk attended,   *promiscuous*
810   Do burn themselves, for having so offended."

811 With this, he breaketh from the sweet embrace
812 Of those fair arms which bound him to her breast,
813 And homeward through the dark laund˙ runs apace,   *pasture*
814 Leaves Love˙ upon her back, deeply distress'd.   *Venus*
815   Look˙ how a bright star shooteth from the sky,   *just as*
816   So glides he in the night from˙ Venus' eye;   *away from*

817 Which after him she darts,˙ as one on shore   *darts her eyes*
*A **friend** who **lately*** 818 Gazing upon a late-embarkèd friend,
embarked *on a ship.* 819 Till the wild waves will have˙ him seen no more,   *allow*
820 Whose ridges˙ with the meeting clouds contend: *wave tops*
821   So˙ did the merciless and pitchy Night   *in this way*
822   Fold˙ in the object that did feed her sight.   *envelop*

823 Whereat˙ amaz'd, as one that unaware — *at which*

824 Hath dropp'd a precious jewel in the flood;

825 Or stonish'd,˙ as night wand'rers often are, — *bewildered*

826 Their light blown out in some mistrustful wood;

827   Even so,˙ confounded in the dark she lay, — *just like this*

828   Having lost the fair discovery of her way.

*Adonis is the one who gave light to her path; he is the **discovery**, or revealer, **of her way**.*

829 And now she beats her heart, whereat it groans,

830 That all the neighbor caves, as seeming troublèd,

831 Make verbal repetition of her moans;

832 Passion˙ on passion deeply is redoublèd: — *lamentation*

833   "Ay me," she cries, and twenty times, "Woe, woe,"

834   And twenty echoes, twenty times cry so.

835 She, marking˙ them, begins a wailing note, — *noticing*

836 And sings extemporally˙ a woeful ditty, — *impromptu*

837 How love makes young men thrall,˙ and old men dote,˙ — *captive; foolish*

838 How love is wise in folly, foolish witty.

839   Her heavy anthem still˙ concludes in woe, — *always*

840   And still the choir of echoes answer so.

841 Her song was tedious, and out-wore the night,

842 For lovers' hours are long, though seeming short.

843 If pleas'd themselves, others, they think, delight

844 In such-like circumstance, with such-like sport.

845   Their copious stories, oftentimes begun,

846   End without audience, and are never done.

847 For who hath she to spend the night withal,

848 But idle sounds resembling parasites˙; — *flattering yes-men*

849 Like shrill-tongu'd tapsters˙ answ'ring every call, — *bartenders*

850 Soothing the humour of fantastic˙ wits.˙ — *capricious; customers*

851   She says, "'Tis so," they answer all, "'Tis so,"

852   And would say after her, if she said "No."

*The **lark** is a symbol of morning.*

853 Lo, here the gentle lark, weary of rest,

854 From his moist˙ cabinet˙ mounts up on high, — *dewy; nest*

855 And wakes the Morning, from whose silver breast

856 The Sun ariseth in his majesty,

*Aurora, the Goddess of **Morning**, wakes Apollo Phoebus, the **Sun** God, from the **silver** water of the Ocean, the "river" that encircles the known world.*

857   Who doth the world so gloriously behold˙ — *face*

858   That cedar tops and hills seem burnish'd gold.

859 Venus salutes him˙ with this fair good morrow: *the Sun God*

860 "O thou clear˙ God, and patron of all light,   *bright & shining*

861 From whom each lamp and shining star doth borrow

862 The beauteous influence that makes him˙ bright,   *a lamp or star*

863   There lives a son˙ that suck'd˙ an earthly mother,   *(Adonis); nursed*

864   May˙ lend thee light, as thou dost lend to other."   *who may*

Influence is an ethereal fluid that streams from the space beyond the Moon and affects things generally, including the character and destiny of humans.

Myrtle trees are sacred to Venus; see page 12.

865 This said, she hasteth to a myrtle grove,

866 Musing the morning is so much o'er-worn,˙   *advanced*

867 And yet she hears no tidings of her love.

868 She harkens for his hounds, and for his horn.˙   *hunting horn*

869   Anon she hears them˙ chant˙ it lustily,   *the hounds; howl*

870   And all in haste she coasteth to the cry.

In hunting, to **coast** *is to run so as to cut off the chased animal.*

871 And as she runs, the bushes in the way,

872 Some catch her by the neck, some kiss her face,

873 Some twine about her thigh to make her stay.

874 She wildly breaketh from their strict embrace,

875   Like a milch˙ doe, whose swelling dugs˙ do ache,   *nursing; udders*

876   Hasting to feed her fawn, hid in some brake.˙   *thicket*

At a bay is when the **hounds** have cornered the prey and the animal turns to make a stand.

877 By this,˙ she hears the hounds are at a bay,   *this time*

878 Whereat she starts, like one that spies an adder

879 Wreath'd up in fatal folds˙ just in his way,   *coils*

880 The fear whereof doth make him˙ shake, and shudder;   *one*

881   Even so,˙ the timorous˙ yelping of the hounds   *just like this; fearful*

882   Appalls˙ her senses, and her spirit confounds.   *enfeebles*

883 For now she knows it is no gentle chase,

884 But the blunt boar, rough bear, or lion proud,

885 Because the cry remaineth in one place,

886 Where fearfully the dogs exclaim aloud,

887   Finding their enemy to be so curst.˙   *vicious*

888   They all strain court'sy who shall cope˙ him first.   *deal with*

They strain courtesy: "You go." "No, you can go first." "No, you can go."

The **heart** *takes all the blood for itself, leaving other organs* **pale** *and* **weak**.

889 This dismal˙ cry rings sadly in her ear,   *disastrous*

890 Through which it enters to surprise˙ her heart,   *attack*

891 Who, overcome by doubt˙ and bloodless fear,   *dread*

892 With cold-pale weakness, numbs each feeling part:

893   Like soldiers, when their captain once doth yield,˙   *give up*

894   They basely fly, and dare not stay the field.˙   *battlefield*

895	Thus stands she in a trembling ecstasy,	*agitation*

*She talks to and **cheers up** her own five **senses**.*

896	Till cheering up her senses all dismay'd,	
897	She tells them 'tis a causeless fantasy	*her five senses*
898	And childish error that they are afraid;	
899	Bids them leave quaking, bids them fear no more —	*stop*
900	And with that word, she spied the hunted boar,	

901	Whose frothy mouth, bepainted all with red,	
902	Like milk and blood being mingl'd both together,	
903	A second fear through all her sinews spread,	
904	Which madly hurries her, she knows not whither.	*to what place*
905	This way she runs, and now she will no further,	
906	But back retires, to rate the boar for murder.	*returns; berate*

907	A thousand spleens bear her a thousand ways;	*impulses*
908	She treads the path that she untreads again;	
909	Her more-than-haste is mated with delays,	*blocked*
910	Like the proceedings of a drunken brain:	
911	Full of respects, yet naught at all respecting;	*considerations*
912	In-hand with all things, naught at all effecting.	*busy*

*The **hound** is hiding, as if safe in its **kennel**.*

913	Here kennel'd in a brake, she finds a hound,	*thicket*
914	And asks the weary caitiff for his Master,	*wretch*
915	And there another licking of his wound,	
916	'Gainst venom'd sores the only sovereign plaster.	*curative*
917	And here she meets another, sadly scowling,	*another hound*
918	To whom she speaks, and he replies with howling.	

***Flap-mouthed** refers to the hanging jowls of **hounds**.*

919	When he hath ceas'd his ill-resounding noise,	
920	Another flap-mouth'd mourner, black and grim,	
921	Against the welkin volleys out his voice;	*sky*
922	Another, and another, answer him,	
923	Clapping their proud tails to the ground below,	
924	Shaking their scratch'd ears, bleeding as they go.	

925	Look how the world's poor people are amazèd,	*just as*
926	At apparitions, signs, and prodigies,	*monstrosities*
927	Whereon with fearful eyes, they long have gazèd,	
928	Infusing them with dreadful prophecies.	

*These **sad signs** Venus worries about are from the **hounds**.*

929	So she at these sad signs, draws up her breath,	
930	And sighing it again, exclaims on Death:	

931	"Hard-favor'd˙ tyrant, ugly, meager, lean,	*unsightly*
932	Hateful divorce˙ of love," thus chides she Death,	*terminator*
933	"Grim-grinning ghost, Earth's worm, what dost thou mean
934	To stifle beauty, and to steal his˙ breath,	*Adonis's*
935	Who, when he liv'd, his breath and beauty set
936	Gloss˙ on the rose, smell to the violet?	*luster*

937	"If he be dead—oh no, it cannot be,˙	*be because*
938	Seeing his beauty, thou shouldst strike at it.
939	Oh yes, it may; thou hast no eyes to see,
940	But hatefully at random dost thou hit.
941	Thy mark˙ is feeble age, but thy false dart	*usual target*
942	Mistakes that aim, and cleaves an infant's heart.

Death, as represented by a skull, has **no eyes** in its sockets.

943	"Hadst thou but bid beware, then he˙ had spoke,	*Adonis*
944	And hearing him, thy power had lost his˙ power.	*its*
945	The Destinies will curse thee for this stroke;
946	They bid thee crop a weed—thou pluck'st a flower.
947	Love's golden arrow at him should have fled,˙	*flown*
948	And not Death's ebon˙ dart to strike him dead.	*black*

949	"Dost thou drink tears, that thou provok'st such weeping?
950	What may a heavy groan advantage thee?
951	Why hast thou cast into eternal sleeping
952	Those eyes that taught all other eyes to see?
953	Now Nature cares˙ not for thy mortal˙ vigor,	*fears; deadly*
954	Since her best work is ruin'd with˙ thy rigor."	*by*

955	Here overcome, as one full of despair,
956	She vail'd˙ her eye-lids, who, like sluices,˙ stopp'd	*lowered; flood-gates*
957	The crystal tide that from her two cheeks fair
958	In the sweet channel˙ of her bosom dropp'd.	*cleavage*
959	But through the flood-gates breaks the silver rain,˙	*tears*
960	And with his˙ strong course˙ opens them again.	*its; current*

*Her **eyes and tears** reflect each other.*

961	O, how her eyes and tears did lend and borrow:
962	Her eye seen in the tears, tears in her eye,
963	Both crystals,˙ where they view'd each other's sorrow;	*reflections*
964	Sorrow, that friendly sighs sought still˙ to dry,	*constantly*
965	But like a stormy day—now wind, now rain—
966	Sighs dry her cheeks, tears make them wet again.

967	Variable passions throng her constant woe,
968	As˙ striving who should best become˙ her grief.
969	All entertain'd,˙ each passion labors so,
970	That every present sorrow seemeth chief,
971	But none is best˙; then join they all together,
972	Like many clouds consulting˙ for foul weather.

as if; suit
admitted
supreme
collaborating

973	By this,˙ far off, she hears some huntsman hallow˙;
974	A nurse's song ne'er pleas'd her babe so well.
975	The dire imagination she did follow,
976	This sound of hope doth labor to expel;
977	For now reviving joy bids her rejoice,
978	And flatters her it˙ is Adonis' voice.

this time; holler
that it

979	Whereat her tears began to turn their tide,
980	Being prison'd in her eye, like pearls in glass,
981	Yet sometimes falls an orient drop beside,
982	Which her cheek melts,˙ as˙ scorning it should pass
983	To wash the foul face of the sluttish ground,
984	Who is but˙ drunken, when she seemeth drown'd.

*The tear drop is **orient**, with the special lustre of a **pearl** of the best quality.*

dries; as if
only

985	O hard-believing˙ love, how strange it seems
986	Not to believe, and yet too˙ credulous:
987	Thy weal˙ and woe are both of them extremes;
988	Despair and hope makes thee ridiculous:
989	The one˙ doth flatter thee in thoughts unlikely;
990	In likely thoughts the other˙ kills thee quickly.

suspicious
too often
well-being
(hope)
(despair)

991	Now she unweaves the web that she hath wrought:
992	Adonis lives, and Death is *not* to blame.
993	It *was* not she that call'd him˙ all too naught˙;
994	Now she adds honors to his hateful name:
995	She clepes˙ him King of Graves, and Grave for Kings,
996	Imperious˙ Sùpreme of all mortal things.

*If only we, Readers, could sometimes **unweave the webs that we have wrought**.*

Death; wicked
names
ruler

997	"No, no," quoth she, "sweet Death, I did but jest.
998	Yet pardon me, I felt a kind of fear
999	When as I met the boar, that bloody beast,
1000	Which knows no pity, but is still˙ severe;
1001	Then, gentle shadow (truth I must confess),
1002	I rail'd on thee, fearing my love's decesse.˙

unceasingly
decease

1003 "'Tis not my fault: the boar provok'd my tongue;
1004 Be wreak'd˙ on him, Invisible Commander.   *revenged*
1005 'Tis he, foul creature, that hath done thee wrong;
1006 I did but act,˙ he's *author* of thy slander.   *act as agent*
1007   Grief hath two˙ tongues, and never woman yet   *a double*
1008   Could rule them both, without ten women's wit."

1009 Thus hoping that Adonis is alive,
1010 Her rash suspect˙ she doth extenuate˙;   *suspicion; excuse*
1011 And that his˙ beauty may the better thrive,   *Adonis's*
1012 With Death she humbly doth insinuate˙:   *ingratiate herself*
1013   Tells him of trophies, statues, tombs, and stories˙   *narrates*
1014   His˙ victories, his triumphs, and his glories.   *Death's*

1015 "O Jove," quoth she, "how much a fool was I,
1016 To be of such a weak and silly mind
1017 To wail his˙ death who lives, and must not die   *Adonis's*
1018 Till mutual˙ overthrow of mortal kind.   *universal*
1019   For he being dead, with him is Beauty slain,
1020   And Beauty dead, black Chaos comes again.

1021 Fie, fie, fond˙ Love, thou art as full of fear   *foolish*
1022 As one with treasure laden, hemm'd with thieves;
1023 Trifles, unwitnessèd with eye or ear,
1024 Thy coward heart with false bethinking grieves."
1025   Even at this word she hears a merry horn,
1026   Whereat she leaps,˙ that˙ was but late forlorn.   *leaps for joy; who*

*Trifles, insignificant things you can't see or hear, grieve your **cowardly heart with false** imaginings.*

1027 As falcon to the lure,˙ away she flies—   *bait*
1028 The grass stoops not, she treads on it so light—
1029 And in her haste, unfortunately spies
1030 The foul boar's conquest on her fair delight,
1031   Which seen, her eyes, as˙ murder'd with the view,   *as if*
1032   Like stars asham'd of˙ day, themselves withdrew;   *by the*

*She sees that the **boar** has indeed killed Adonis, **her fair delight.***

1033 Or as the snail, whose tender horns being hit,
1034 Shrinks backward in his shelly cave with pain,
1035 And there, all smother'd up, in shade˙ doth sit,   *darkness*
1036 Long after fearing to creep forth again:
1037   So,˙ at his bloody view, her eyes are fled   *just like that*
1038   Into the deep-dark cabins of her head,

1039	Where they resign their office, and their light,	*duties*
1040	To the disposing of her troubl'd Brain,	*direction*
1041	Who bids them still consort with ugly Night,	*her eyes; remain*
1042	And never wound the Heart with looks again—	
1043	Who, like a king perplexèd in his throne,	*the Heart*
1044	By their suggestion, gives a deadly groan.	*the eyes'; incitement*

1045	Whereat each tributary subject quakes,	*subordinate; organ*
1046	As when the wind, imprison'd in the ground,	
1047	Struggling for passage, Earth's foundation shakes,	
1048	Which with cold terror, doth men's minds confound.	*stupefy*
1049	This mutiny each part doth so surprise	*body part; suddenly attack*
1050	That from their dark beds once more leap her eyes,	

*Elizabethans thought earthquakes were a result of **wind** trapped in the **Earth**.*

1051	And being open'd, threw unwilling light	
1052	Upon the wide wound that the boar had trench'd	
1053	In his soft flank, whose wonted lily white,	*Adonis's; customary*
1054	With purple tears that his wound wept, had drench'd.	
1055	No flower was nigh, no grass, herb, leaf, or weed,	
1056	But stole his blood, and seem'd with him to bleed.	*but did*

1057	This solemn sympathy, poor Venus noteth;	
1058	Over one shoulder doth she hang her head.	
1059	Dumbly she passions, franticly she doteth;	*shows her grief*
1060	She thinks he could not die, he is not dead.	
1061	Her voice is stopp'd, her joints forget to bow;	
1062	Her eyes are mad, that they have wept till now.	*for lesser cause before*

1063	Upon his hurt she looks so steadfastly	
1064	That her sight, dazzling, makes the wound seem three,	*dizzying her*
1065	And then she reprehends her mangling eye,	*reprimands*
1066	That makes more gashes where no breach should be:	
1067	His face seems twain, each several limb is doublèd,	*individual*
1068	For oft the eye mistakes, the brain being troublèd.	

*She scolds her **eye** which visually **mangles** the wound and makes it look like **more gashes**.*

1069	"My tongue cannot express my grief for one,	
1070	And yet," quoth she, "behold two Àdons dead.	
1071	My sighs are blown away, my salt tears gone;	
1072	Mine eyes are turn'd to fire, my heart to lead—	
1073	Heavy heart's lead, melt at mine eyes' red fire;	
1074	So shall I die by drops of hot desire.	*in this same way*

*"My **leaden heart** will **melt** from the **red fire-hot tears**, then I will die by the same **drops**."*

1075	"Alas, poor world, what treasure hast thou lost;
1076	What face remains alive that's worth the viewing?
1077	Whose tongue is music now? What canst thou boast
1078	Of things long since,˙ or any thing ensuing˙?	*past; to come*
1079	The flowers are sweet, their colors fresh and trim,
1080	But true sweet beauty liv'd and died with him.˙	*Adonis*

*Venus wants no one, **no creature**, to wear a **bonnet nor veil** to protect their skin since no one else is beautiful (except Adonis), but the **Wind** and **Sun** don't even want to bother with you anyway.*

1081	"Bonnet nor veil, henceforth˙ no creature wear;	*from here on out*
1082	Nor˙ Sun, nor Wind, will ever strive to kiss you:	*neither*
1083	Having no fair˙ to lose, you need not fear;	*beauty*
1084	The Sun doth scorn you, and the Wind doth hiss you.
1085	But when Adonis liv'd, Sun and sharp Air
1086	Lurk'd like two thieves, to rob him of his fair.

1087	"And therefore˙ would he put his bonnet on,	*for that reason*
1088	Under whose brim the gaudy Sun would peep;
1089	The Wind would blow it off, and being˙ gone,	*his hat being*
1090	Play with his locks; then would Adonis weep,
1091	And straight,˙ in pity of his tender years,	*immediately*
1092	They˙ both would strive who first should dry his tears.	*Sun & Wind*

1093	"To see his face, the lion walk'd along
1094	Behind some hedge, because he would not fear˙ him;	*frighten*
1095	To rècreate˙ himself when he hath song,	*entertain*
1096	The tiger would be tame, and gently hear him;
1097	If he had spoke, the wolf would leave his prey,
1098	And never fright the silly˙ lamb that day.	*innocent*

1099	"When he˙ beheld his shadow˙ in the brook,	*Adonis; reflection*
1100	The fishes spread on it their golden gills;
1101	When he was by, the birds such pleasure took
1102	That some would sing, some other in their bills˙	*beaks*
1103	Would bring him mulberries and ripe-red cherries;
1104	He fed them with his sight, they him with berries.

1105	"But this foul, grim, and urchin-snouted boar,
1106	Whose downward eye still˙ looketh for a grave,	*constantly*
1107	Ne'er saw the beauteous livery that he˙ wore—	*Adonis*
1108	Witness the entertainment˙ that he˙ gave.	*treatment; the boar*
1109	If he˙ did see his face, why then I know	*the boar*
1110	He˙ thought to kiss him,˙ and hath kill'd him so.	*the boar; Adonis*

1111	"'Tis true, 'tis true, thus˙ was Adonis slain:	*in this way*
1112	He ran upon the boar with his sharp spear,	
1113	Who did not whet his teeth at him again,˙	*in return*
1114	But by a kiss, thought to persuade˙ him there,	*win over*
1115	And nuzzling in his flank, the loving swine	
1116	Sheath'd unaware the tusk in his soft groin.	

1117	"Had I been tooth'd like him, I must confess,	
1118	With kissing him I should have kill'd him first;	
1119	But he is dead, and never did he bless	
1120	My youth with his — the more am I accurs'd."	
1121	With this, she falleth in the place she stood,	
1122	And stains her face with his congealèd blood.	

*A **coffer** is a treasure chest, so Adonis's eyes are in two treasure chests. (Her own **eyes are fled into the deep-dark cabins of her head,** lines 1037–1038.)*

1123	She looks upon his lips, and they are pale;	
1124	She takes him by the hand, and that is cold;	
1125	She whispers in his ears, a heavy˙ tale,	*sorrowful*
1126	As if they heard the woeful words she told.	
1127	She lifts the coffer-lids that close his eyes,	
1128	Where lo, two lamps˙ burnt out, in darkness lies;	*eyes*

1129	Two glasses,˙ where her self, her self beheld	*mirrors of his eyes*
1130	A thousand times, and now no more reflect,	
1131	Their virtue˙ lost, wherein they late excell'd,	*power to see*
1132	And every beauty robb'd of his˙ effect.	*its*
1133	"Wonder of Time," quoth she, "this is my spite,˙	*vexation*
1134	That thou being dead, the day should yet be light.	

*Beginning here and in the following four stanzas, the word **It** refers to **love.** Venus curses love for all the rest of us.*

1135	"Since thou art dead, lo, here I prophesy:	
1136	Sorrow on love hereafter shall attend;	
1137	It˙ shall be waited on with˙ Jealousy,	*Love; by*
1138	Find sweet beginning, but unsavory end;	
1139	Ne'er settled equally, but high or low,˙	*high or low social rank*
1140	That all love's pleasure shall not match his˙ woe.	*its*

1141	"It shall be fickle, false, and full of fraud,	
1142	Bud and be blasted˙ in a breathing while˙;	*withered; moment*
1143	The bottom poison, and the top o'er-straw'd˙	*over-strewn*
1144	With sweets, that˙ shall the truest sight beguile.˙	*so that; deceive*
1145	The strongest body shall it make most weak,	
1146	Strike the wise dumb,˙ and teach the fool to speak.	*mute*

1147	"It shall be sparing,˙ and too full of riot,˙	*stingy; excess*
1148	Teaching decrepit age to tread˙ the measures;	*dance*
1149	The staring˙ ruffian shall it keep in quiet,	*glaring*
1150	Pluck down the rich, enrich the poor with treasures;	
1151	It shall be raging mad, and silly˙ mild;	*feebly*
1152	Make the young old, the old become a child.	

1153	"It shall suspect where is no cause of fear;	
1154	It shall not fear where it should most mistrust;	
1155	It shall be merciful, and too severe,	
1156	And most deceiving when it seems most just˙;	*trustworthy*
1157	Perverse it shall be, where it shows most toward˙;	*submissive*
1158	Put fear to valor, courage to the coward.	

1159	"It shall be cause of war and dire events,	
1160	And set dissension 'twixt the son and sire,	
1161	Subject˙ and servile˙ to all discontents,	*cause; slave*
1162	As dry combustious matter is to fire.	
1163	Sith˙ in his prime, Death doth my love destroy,	*since*
1164	They that love best, their loves shall not enjoy."	

1165	By this,˙ the boy that by her side lay kill'd	*this time*
1166	Was melted like a vapor from her sight,	
1167	And in his blood that on the ground lay spill'd,	
1168	A purple flower sprung up, checker'd with white,	
1169	Resembling well his pale cheeks, and the blood	
1170	Which in round drops upon their whiteness stood.	

*Traditionally, the **flower** is an anemone.*

1171	She bows her head, the new-sprung flower to smell,	
1172	Comparing it to her Adonis' breath,	
1173	And says within her bosom it shall dwell,	
1174	Since he himself is reft˙ from her by Death.	*torn*
1175	She crops the stalk, and in the breach˙ appears	*cut end*
1176	Green-dropping sap, which she compares to tears.	

Every little grief made Adonis weep.

1177	"Poor flower," quoth she, "this was thy father's˙ guise—	*Adonis's*
1178	Sweet issue of a more sweet-smelling sire—	
1179	For every little grief to wet his eye;	
1180	To grow˙ unto himself was his desire,	*mature*
1181	And so 'tis thine; but know, it is as good	
1182	To wither in my breast as in his blood.	

1183 "Here was thy father's˙ bed, here in my breast;   *Adonis's*

1184 Thou art the next of blood,˙ and 'tis thy right.   *kin*

1185 Lo, in this hollow cradle˙ take thy rest;   *cleavage*

1186 My throbbing heart shall rock thee day and night.

1187   There shall not be one minute in an hour

1188   Wherein I will not kiss my sweet love's flower."

1189 Thus, weary of the world, away she hies˙   *hastens*

1190 And yokes her silver doves, by whose swift aid

1191 Their mistress, mounted, through the empty skies

1192 In her light chariot, quickly is convey'd,

Paphos, *home of Venus,* 1193   Holding their course to Paphos, where their Queen
is on the island of Cyprus. 1194   Means to immure˙ her self, and not be seen.   *imprison*

Finis

50

ADONIS TRANSFORMED • Ovid, *The Metamorphoses, Book Ten*

This is the English version Shakespeare would have known, translated by Arthur Golding and published in 1567. Shakespeare could also have read Ovid's original Latin, as well as other ancient versions of the story. Golding wrote this in "fourteeners," fourteen syllables, as was common for epic poems at the time.

1 This warning given, with yokèd swannes away through aire she goth.
2 But manhod by admonishment restreynèd could not bee.
3 By chaunce his hounds in following of the tracke, a Boare did see,
4 And rowsèd him. And as the swyne was comming from the wood,
5 Adonis hit him with a dart askew, and drew the blood.
6 The Boare streyght with his hookèd groyne the hunting staffe out drew
7 Bestaynèd with his blood, and on Adonis did pursew,
8 Who trembling and retyring back, to place of refuge drew.

His cods are his testicles.

9 And hyding in his codds his tuskes as farre as he could thrust,
10 He layd him all along for dead upon the yellow dust.
11 Dame Venus in her chariot draw'n with swannes was scarce arriv'd
12 At Cyprus, when shee knew afarre the sygh of him depryv'd

Cygnets are young swans.

13 Of lyfe. Shee turnd her Cygnets backe and when shee from the skye
14 Beehilld him dead, and in his blood bewltred for to lye:
15 Shee leapèd downe, and tare at once hir garments from her brist,
16 And rent her heare, and beate upon her stomack with her fist,
17 And blaming sore the Destnyes, sayd: Yit shall they not obteine
18 Their will in all things. Of my greefe remembrance shall remayne
19 (Adonis) whyle the world doth last. From yeere to yeere shall growe
20 A thing that of my heavinesse and of thy death shall showe
21 The lively likenesse. In a flowre thy blood I will bestowe.

*When **Persephone** was living with Hades in the Underworld, she got jealous of **Minthe** for sleeping with her husband, stomped on **Minthe,** and turned her into the **mint** plant.*

22 Hadst thou the powre, Persephonee, rank-sented Mints to make
23 Of womens limbes? and may not I lyke powre upon mee take
24 Without disdeine and spyght, to turne Adonis to a flowre?
25 This sed, shee sprinckl'd Nectar on the blood, which through the powre
26 Therof did swell like bubbles sheere that ryse in weather cleere
27 On water. And before that full an howre expyrèd weere,
28 Of all one color with the blood a flowre she there did fynd
29 Even like the flowre of that same tree whose frute in tender rynde
30 Have pleasant graynes inclosde. Howbee't the use of them is short.
31 For why the leaves do hang so looce through lightnesse in such sort,
32 As that the windes that all things perce, with every little blast
33 Doo shake them off and shed them so as that they cannot last.

ADONIS TRANSFORMED • Ovid, *The Metamorphoses, Book Ten*

This version is translated from the Latin by Brookes More, 1922.
It is in iambic pentameter, ten syllables, as is Shakespeare's version.
Available in the public domain at www.perseus.tufts.edu.

1   Indeed she warn'd him.
2   Harnessing her swans,
3   She travel'd swiftly through the yielding air;
4   But his rash courage would not heed advice.
5   By chance his dogs, which follow'd a sure track,
6   Arous'd a wild boar from his hiding place;
7   And, as he rush'd out from his forest lair,
8   Adonis pierced him with a glancing stroke.
9   Infuriate, the fierce boar's curvèd snout
10 First struck the spear-shaft from his bleeding side;
11 And while the trembling youth was seeking where
12 To find a safe retreat, the savage beast
13 Raced after him, until at last he sank
14 His deadly tusk deep in Adonis' groin,
15 And stretched him dying on the yellow sand.

Aphrodite is the Greek name for Venus.

16 And now sweet Aphrodite, borne through air
17 In her light chariot, had not yet arriv'd
18 At Cyprus, on the wings of her white swans.
19 Afar she recogniz'd his dying groans,
20 And turn'd her white birds towards the sound. And when
21 Down looking from the lofty sky, she saw
22 Him nearly dead, his body bath'd in blood,
23 She leap'd down—tore her garment—tore her hair —
24 And beat her bosom with distracted hands.
25 And blaming Fate, said, "But not everything
26 Is at the mercy of your cruèl power.
27 My sorrow for Adonis will remain,
28 Enduring as a lasting monument.
29 Each passing year the memory of his death
30 Shall cause an imitation of my grief.

*When **Persephone** was living with Hades in the Underworld, she got jealous of **Minthe** for sleeping with her husband, stomped on **Minthe,** and turned her into the **mint** plant.*

31 "Your blood, Adonis, will become a flower
32 Perennial. Was it not allow'd to you,
33 Persephone, to transform Minthe's limbs
34 Into sweet fragrant mint? And can this change
35 Of my lov'd hero be denied to me?"

36 Her grief declar'd, she sprinklèd his blood with
37 Sweet-smelling nectar, and his blood as soon
38 As touch'd by it began to effervesce,
39 Just as transparent bubbles always rise
40 In rainy weather. Nor was there a pause
41 More than an hour, when from Adonis' blood,
42 Exactly of its color, a lovèd flower
43 Sprang up, such as pom'granates give to us,
44 Small trees which later hide their seeds beneath
45 A tough rind. But the joy it gives to man
46 Is short-liv'd, for the winds which give the flower
47 Its name, Anemone, shake it right down,
48 Because its slender hold, always so weak,
49 Lets it fall to the ground from its frail stem.

Your notes

iREAD
SHAKESPEARE
out loud and in community!

Check the web site at **iReadShakespeare.org** for other Readers' Editions, as well as great support material for your reading group.

Colophon

The main font used in this book is **Archer**, with *Desire* for the large headlines.

The book was designed in Adobe InDesign.

Printed in Great Britain
by Amazon